CONSTABLE BY THE SEA

CONSTABLE BY THE SEA

Nicholas Rhea

ROBERT HALE · LONDON

Robert Hale Limited
Clerkenwell House
Clerkenwell Green
London ECIR 0HT

Rhea, Nicholas
Constable by the sea.
1. Police——England——North Yorkshire——
History——20th century
Rn: Peter Norman Walker   I. Title
363.2'092'4   HV8196.A5N/

ISBN 0–7090–2380–4

Photoset in Plantin by
Kelly Typesetting Limited
Bradford-on-Avon, Wiltshire
Printed in Great Britain by
St Edmundsbury Press
Bury St Edmunds, Suffolk and
bound by W.B.C. Bookbinders Limited

1

And the sun went down
And the stars came out far over the summer sea.
Alfred, Lord Tennyson, 1809–92

It was the first week of July and I was on a slow train which was carrying me to the seaside. Mine was not a holiday trip, however, but a police duty engagement. I was on my way to Strensford, a picturesque and sometimes busy seaside resort on the north-east coast of Yorkshire. Graced by miles of smooth, yellow sand, Strensford is famed for its kippers and the fact that the bright summer sun both rises and sets over the sea. It is also known for its towering cliffs with a ruined abbey gloriously perched on top, and the haphazard cluster of red-roofed cottages which crowd around the harbour side, at times touching the water.

A few years ago, I had started my police career in this town, but much as I liked Strensford, I hadn't volunteered for this return visit. Who would volunteer to leave behind a loving wife and four tiny children? It is at times like this policemen realize that their wives are angels and models of patience and understanding – well, most of them are!

It was Sergeant Blaketon who had said, 'Rhea, I put your name down for coastal duties. You could do with a change of scenery and the chance to do some real police work; it'll do you good to cope with daft holiday-makers, drunken locals and masses of cars all heading for the same parking space. So I've volunteered you for this duty. Fourteen weeks, it is. Each spell of duty is seven days on followed by two days off. You'll be working shifts, so you'll get home once in a while.

'You'll be in uniform, helping the local lads to cope with the summer rush. Report at Strensford Police Station prompt at 9 a.m. a week on Monday, and take enough stuff to last you a week. Digs will be found and food will be provided. It'll be no holiday, mind you, so don't go thinking it's a doddle.'

It didn't matter whether or not I wanted to volunteer – I was on my way, but one thing did please me. For three blissful months or so, I'd be free from the domineering presence of Sergeant Oscar Blaketon. That pleasing thought was the one bright spot in the gloom which would follow departure from my little family.

I was familiar with the coastal problems. I'd served my police apprenticeship at Strensford and knew that during the winter months the town literally died. Lashed by fierce north-east gales, high seas, dense fogs and intensely cold weather, the little resort simply ceased to appeal to anyone. Even its own residents grumbled about the treatment it received from the uncaring weather. As the claws of winter chased away the holiday-makers, Strensford's streets and hotels emptied, its beaches became deserted and its shops closed their doors against the Arctic blasts. To walk those blustery streets on a Sunday in winter was tantamount to trekking to the North Pole.

This was in direct contrast to the summer months, when the town changed beyond all belief (even the fogs were a few degrees warmer). Holiday-makers swamped the place. Boarding houses and hotels re-opened, the amusement arcades dusted their machines, camping sites bustled with activity and the shopkeepers gave their premises a new coat of paint. Lines of traffic flooded into the town; bus-loads came for the day and train-loads came for longer periods.

Even foreigners came to Strensford in the summer. Flat-capped folks came from the West Riding of Yorkshire, and beer-swilling Geordies came down from the north. Scots folks arrived for two-week stretches to spend a little cash, Europeans passed through, and it was even rumoured that some from the south of England ventured this far north.

And as if to please all those visitors, the sun occasionally broke through the summer fogs to bathe the town in a warm, pleasing glow.

From the police officer's point of view, this annual influx presented severe problems. In the winter, the resident constables were bored out of their minds due to a lamentable lack of activity, whereas the hectic summer months pushed them to their limits and beyond. There just weren't sufficient officers to cope with the plethora of problems the visitors managed to generate.

It is widely known in police circles that when people descend *en masse* upon a place, they produce problems. Those problems are bewildering and awesome in their range and complexity, and it is invariably the police who have to deal with them. At the seaside, they range from simple things like children getting lost or vehicles travelling the wrong way along one-way streets, to mammoth worries like people leaping off cliffs to end their lives or ships going down with all hands. The coastal constable sees a lot, learns a lot, copes with a lot and, in despair and disbelief, shakes his head a lot.

I was aware of all these factors as my train neared the end of its journey. I was to become, however temporarily, such a constable. For the next few weeks, which embraced the height of Strensford's summer season, I was to be a constable by the sea.

After a very early morning start, I had caught this train, the only one which would allow me to arrive at Strensford Police Station by no later than the stipulated hour of 9 a.m. This train was also the school-train, for on its long tortuous but incredibly picturesque route through the Strensbeck Valley of the North York Moors, it gathered masses of children from the dales and villages and poured them into Strensford to be 'eddicated' as the dalesmen put it. Once in town, they dispersed daily to their secondary schools or to the grammar school.

In those days, railway carriages were divided into individual compartments, each of which seated about ten people, and so I had entered one which contained nothing that looked remotely like a rampant schoolchild. Schoolchildren can be very wearisome as travelling companions. Instead, my fellow passengers were a sober bunch of people from the villages, people whose livelihood was earned in Strensford through earnest toil in its shops, offices and factories. As I'd entered, they had stared at me briefly; for one thing, I was a stranger on the train, and secondly, my mode of dress was an obvious mixture of civilian clothing and police uniform.

I had deemed this necessary because I had to be at the police station no later than 9 a.m., and the train arrived at Strensford at five minutes to nine. This meant I had no time to change, so to save time, and to prevent a possible disciplinary charge by being late, I had donned my best uniform and wore it beneath a civilian mackintosh. Thus I sported large black, polished boots, dark blue serge trousers, a blue shirt and black tie, all of which were clearly visible and which announced that I was a member of the Force. My tunic was nicely concealed beneath my raincoat, while my hand luggage comprised a bulky holdall, a small suitcase and some bags of assorted necessities.

One snag was that police uniforms are the most difficult things to pack, consequently my cumbersome greatcoat was slung on top of my holdall, between the handles, and for the time being my police cap on top of that. These were all on the rack above my head. I had a second tunic slung over my suitcase and had other bags and belongings draped around it. I reasoned that, even though my luggage was bulky and a nuisance, I could cope with it during the short, brisk walk from the railway station.

Sergeant Blaketon reckoned it was only a two-minute walk, but I knew the train could be late. Fortunately, this one was on time, but even so, I would have no moments to spare once the train halted at Strensford. Believing in early preparation, I stood up and began to gather my belongings as it rattled beneath the huge viaduct on its final mile or so. I was determined to have my things off the racks and securely clutched in my hands by the time the train halted. Then I'd make a dash for the barrier with my ticket at the ready, and I would gain the town's streets before the other passengers clogged the exit.

'Ah wouldn't bother,' said a man in the corner opposite.

'Pardon?' I wasn't sure he was addressing me.

'Ah said Ah wouldn't bother,' he was pointing at my unwieldy collection of belongings. 'Getting them things down yet. You'll not beat 'em.'

'Beat 'em?' I suspended my work and placed one hand on the edge of the rack as I questioned him.

'Aye,' he said. 'The kids. Schoolkids. They'll be out afore you, like a horde of bloody rampaging cattle, they are. It's a bloody stampede. We allus sit tight till they've got clear. It's safer in the long run.'

The other passengers clearly agreed with this middle-aged chap in the sports jacket, for they nodded and smiled at his words of common sense. But I couldn't afford to wait – it was already six minutes to nine.

'Thanks,' I smiled at them all, and at him in particular. 'But I've got to be at work prompt at nine o'clock, not a second later. I'll get through the crush. But thanks for the warning.'

After all, I told myself, I had been in the RAF during my National Service, and that experience had taught me a lot about rushing for trains, rushing off trains, galloping heavily laden along busy platforms, changing stations with seconds to spare, battling through rush-hour crowds – we servicemen had done it all, and that expertise was going to be my salvation this very morning.

I stood at the carriage door and lowered the window so that I could operate the catch from the outside. As I did so, I breathed in the clean salt air, air which some believe contains ozone but which in fact is a heady mixture of evaporating brine and kipper smoke. Even so, the blast of fresh air which blew into my face and ruffled my hair had a definite tang of the wide-open sea. It was clean and refreshing, beautifully pure and enervating. It held a promise of excitement and romance.

We were now reducing speed; the train had arrived at the outward end of the long, curving platform and was braking. There was the clash of brakes, the squeal of iron wheels on iron rails, the clanking of buffers all accompanied by the shuddering motions of a heavily laden train being forced to a halt. We entered the station buildings, and the roof appeared in view; slowly, we cruised to a halt.

Quickly, I opened my door. The train was still moving, albeit very, very slowly. I gripped my assorted baggage just as I wanted it, and I could see the deserted barrier near the head of the train. There was no reason why I should not be first through. A forlorn ticket-collector stood there, his dark blue uniform prominent against the greyness of the station's stonework, and there was no one ahead of me. The way was clear.

With my customary agility and my practised RAF leap, I descended from the still-moving train, and in spite of my luggage, my legs had no trouble adjusting to a rapid running motion. I was on my way, and my luggage bobbed and bounced as I ran. I was running towards the ticket-collector at the speed of the slowing train. I could see him waiting for me, even though he did seem to be an awful long way off.

I'm not sure what went wrong with my strategy.

I became aware that I was being rapidly overtaken and simultaneously surrounded by noisy, galloping schoolchildren. Hats, scarfs, satchels, waving arms and bare knees were all about me, all heading in the same direction but with even more speed and urgency than I could muster. I was vaguely aware of countless stomping feet, many shrill voices all raised in unison and an unseen determination by each one of them to be first through that ticket-barrier. I was probably unwittingly involved in a daily race for some kind of momentary, childish glory.

I was unavoidably swept along by the thrusting crowd; this was mass movement at its very worst, for even if I'd wished to turn around, it would have been impossible. I had no choice but to go along with the stampeding mass of school-bound youngsters, and as I galloped along with them, I realized that they had also to be in class by nine o'clock.

To add to my impending and inevitable delay at the barrier, my uniform greatcoat, which had been lying on top of my holdall, had gradually slipped, and its tail was trailing on the platform. It was gathering dust as I ran, and with horror I realized that my cap was also working loose. Being swept along as I was, I could not halt my onward rush to rectify matters.

And as these doom-laden realizations impressed themselves upon me, disaster arrived. As I pumped my way through the crowd, I trod upon that loose coat tail. My running motion was rudely interrupted and I was launched briefly into mid-air, then went sprawling to earth in an entanglement of arms and legs, some of which did not belong to me. As I fell, I lost my grip on the holdall; I recall that it bounded, or was kicked, from my grasp, and it disappeared among hundreds of stamping feet as it was bundled along by the moving mass. My cap broke loose too and went bowling along beneath a tumult of feet as I lay on the platform with a multiplicity of shoes pounding my back, head, arms and legs. The surging crowd moved on. I tried to get up; I couldn't. Each time, more feet pounded me back into the ground. And then, quite suddenly, it was all over and there was peace.

I struggled to my feet and saw that a mass of children had come to a halt around the unfortunate ticket-collector, but their number was reducing rapidly as they squeezed through the barriers and ran for their waiting buses or hurried to their schools.

My battered holdall was lying midway between me and the barrier, and my trampled greatcoat was spread open nearby, something like Walter Raleigh's famous cape, except there was no royal personage to walk upon it and no puddle to justify its position on the ground. It was smothered in the thick grey dust of the railway station.

I had no idea where my cap had gone.

I dusted down my trousers and mackintosh and then began to make my slow, somewhat painful way to the barrier, retrieving my holdall and greatcoat *en route*. I got there eventually, by which time the last of the children had passed through. Their disappearance through the narrow gap was rather like sand slipping through an hourglass, and their final departure produced an air of sudden peace and tranquillity.

'Your cap,' grunted the ticket collector. It was perched on the gatepost at the barrier, buckled, bruised and very dirty. 'They're animals, the lot of 'em. Bloody animals. No respect.'

I smiled ruefully as I handed in my ticket and lifted my cap from its temporary resting place. As I did so, I became aware of a man behind me.

11

'Ah said thoo shouldn't have bothered.' It was the man from the railway carriage, and he was shaking his head. 'Thoo hasn't saved any time. See? We've caught thoo up.'

Through the gap in the wall which was the exit, I could see the police station, a red-brick building on a hill about four hundred yards away. The ticket-collector noticed me looking anxiously at it.

'By lad,' he said. 'You'll need a bit more about you if you're going to be stationed in this spot! 'Specially with summer coming on. Some o' these day-trippers eat young lads like you! Now, next time, stay on this train till yon school-rush is clear of this barrier.'

'Ah did warn you,' muttered the fellow in the sports jacket, and now I could see the other passengers heading this way.

'Thanks.' I tried to show pleasure at their helpfulness, but my back hurt and I felt a real mess.

It was one minute to nine as I left the portals of the railway station, and I struggled across the street with my battered load. I took a short cut across the forecourt of the bus station, hurried through a back street near a cinema and climbed the short, steep, cobbled hill towards the red-brick edifice which was Strensford's police station, a building erected in Victoria's reign.

I was puffing and panting by now, with sweat pouring off me. My perspiration had gathered a good deal of flying dust during my tumble, and I knew my hands and face were stained and dirty. My hair was hanging limp and I could feel the mess I was in. My cumbersome baggage had made things worse. Items trailed from it, my cap kept falling off, and the infuriating coat insisted on slipping to the ground.

Eventually I arrived at the entrance, which was along a level cul-de-sac, a side-street leading off the cobbled hill, and which was marked by a blue sign saying 'Police'. There was a row of bicycles parked against the wall but no outward sign of activity.

I entered to memories of my early days here and hurriedly descended a dark flight of steps into the ageing bowels of this curious old place. I found myself at the hatch over which was a notice saying, 'Enquiries'. I peeped through – there was an office full of policemen, so I walked in as I'd done much less confidently a few years ago.

'Rhea!' bellowed an all-too-familiar voice in my ear. 'You're late! Three minutes late on your first day's duty. And look at the state of you! Has there been a train crash? Have you been fighting drunks already, Rhea? And that uniform! And you should not be wearing a mixture of civilian clothes with your uniform . . .'

Sergeant Blaketon had also come to Strensford for a spell of coastal duty. I let him ramble on but did wonder how he had managed to arrive on time and why he had not brought me with him. I was to learn later that he had instructed one of the Ashfordly constables to drive him over in the official car, a privilege not permitted constables. Man and car had returned to patrol duties around my peaceful patch at Aidensfield.

'You're on nights, tonight, Rhea,' Sergeant Blaketon was saying. 'So you needn't have got dressed up like that. Now, your digs are at the Breckdale Private Hotel across the street. Go there now. The rest have already arrived. Settle in, they'll explain things to you, then report back here for duty at ten tonight. And Rhea, be smart and be on time. In fact, be early. Ten minutes to ten, on the dot.'

'Yes, sergeant.' Quite suddenly, I wasn't looking forward to being a constable by the sea.

My first night's duty wasn't too bad. I knew my way around the town and had no real difficulty adjusting to this changed routine. Even so, there was a marked contrast between plodding a beat around farms and villages and treading featureless streets. Now my time would be spent visiting public houses to quell any possible fighting and to ensure they closed on time, or checking numerous shop doors to make sure they were locked and secure against prowling criminals.

It was the latter task which almost landed me in more hot water with Sergeant Blaketon; the incident occurred during my second night on duty.

By way of an excuse, I ought to add that I had been very tired even before embarking on that second tour of eight footslogging hours. Having arrived at nine o'clock on that Monday morning, I had been awake all that day and, without any sleep, had performed an eight-hour tour of night duty that night. I'd collapsed into bed just after 6.30 the following morning but had not slept at all. For one thing, I missed Mary; for another, a strange bed was not conducive to peaceful slumber, and the routine sounds of the hotel were not the best at lulling me to sleep. Finally, I was called down to lunch at one o'clock, so my sleep total was practically nil. It was not the best recipe for another tour of night duty.

When I began that second tour, therefore, I was almost asleep on my feet even before parading for duty and put on what I hoped was a wide-awake appearance during the briefing in the muster room. Sergeant Blaketon was duty sergeant that night, and I caught him eyeing me once or twice as he informed us about the night's work. There were unoccupied houses and shops to care for, likely trouble-spots outside dance halls and clubs, and a spate of burglaries by villains using stolen cars.

'Are you all right, Rhea?' he suddenly asked.

'Yes, sergeant,' I said, looking puzzled.

'You look bloody awful,' he commented. 'Pale and tired. Is this townie style of bobbying too much for you?'

'Not at all!' I tried to sound very confident in my response. 'I'm fine.'

'Right,' he addressed the entire complement of tonight's officers. 'To your beats.'

I had been allocated No. 2 Beat, which comprised the town centre, and this meant I had lots of shop premises, office blocks, restaurants and pubs to check during the first half of my tour. Those mundane tasks would pass the time rapidly until my 2 a.m. break.

To be honest, those first four hours flew past; I was so busy checking all the property for which I was responsible that I had no time to feel tired. This was aided by cheery home-going drinkers who always stopped for a chat with the patrolling policeman. Their good humour helped to while away the long night hours – as long as they were not troublesome. It is fair to say that very few of them did cause real trouble – we would often place a cheerful drunk into a taxi to help him home, the 'penalty' being the taxi-fare, but they rarely caused anything more serious.

At 2 a.m., therefore, I adjourned to the station, where I thoroughly enjoyed my sandwiches and coffee.

The worst was to come. The second half of a night shift is always a trial because, even with an adequate amount of sleep, there is that awful period between 3 a.m. and 4 a.m. when the patrolling constable is at his lowest ebb. There are times when he is literally asleep on his feet, when he is walking like a robot, when he is not seeing anything and when he doesn't know anything. It is a ghastly time and few escape it. Having been denied my fair share of sleep, that low ebb hit me hard. I was patrolling the second half of my beat, refreshed with coffee and sandwiches, and the time had reached 3 a.m. Daylight was not far away. But at five minutes past three, by now feeling exceedingly weary, I found an insecure shop door. It was not locked, although the shop lights were out and there did not appear to have been a break-in. I checked all the external windows and the back door, but it became clear that the shop-keeper had forgotten to lock his front door.

This discovery kept me awake for a while, and I knew my next task was to search the shop for intruders. This was in the days before police officers enjoyed the support of personal radio sets, so I was alone. Snapping on my powerful torch, I entered the shop and began a thorough search in the darkness. It was a furniture shop on two storeys, and I made a meticulous search of every conceivable hiding place. There was no intruder, the till had not been forced and there did not appear to have been a break-in.

The simple solution was to lock the offending door by dropping the latch, and then get the key-holder out of bed to ask for a check of his premises. This was always done, just to be sure that all was well. This rude awakening had the added effect of making the key-holder more careful in the future about locking up. But this lock was of the mortice type, and there was no key in the lock. I could not leave the premises insecure – there might be a shop-breaker lurking in the night, so I picked up the shop's telephone and rang the police station.

Sergeant Blaketon answered.

He listened to my story then said, 'Right, Rhea, I've checked the key-holders' register and that furniture shop belongs to a chap called Raymond Austin. He lives out at Oakdale, and that's a good half-hour's drive, then he's got to get dressed. I'll ring him now and get him to lock his shop. You wait there until he comes – it could be three-quarters of an hour; check it all over just to be sure nothing's been stolen, and then make sure he locks up.'

'Yes, sergeant.' I replaced the telephone and resigned myself to a long wait. But there was one advantage about having to wait here – it was a furniture shop full of comfortable seats.

I closed the front door but did not switch on the shop's lights and with the aid of my torch selected a comfortable settee upon which to wait. It was nicely out of view of the windows—not that many folks would be passing by or window-shopping at this time of the morning, but I did not wish to be stared at during my lonely vigil. I settled down on the lovely soft surface of the settee, and in the warmth of the evening my eyes began to close and my head began to nod. My head jolted alarmingly as I fought to keep awake, and in an effort to do so, I walked around the shop once or twice, but the inevitable happened. Eventually, I fell fast asleep.

When I awoke, daylight had arrived. The summer dawn arrived early on the coast, and when I checked my watch, it was four o'clock. Four o'clock? It took me a few minutes to gather my wits and to realize where I was, but then I recalled with horror that I was still in the shop and that I must have nodded off. I hurriedly left my cosy resting-place, shivered and walked around for a minute or two, checking the time and wondering where the key-holder was. Surely it was time he was here! If there'd been a problem, Sergeant Blaketon would have rung back.

I decided to have a look up the street, just to see if he was anywhere in sight. I went to the front door. It was locked. I shook it, I tugged it, I hauled on the handle, but it was as secure as a fortress.

With my heart sinking fast into my boots, I realized what had happened. Mr Austin must have driven down from Oakdale and arrived at his premises while I was slumbering out of his sight; he'd simply locked his door and departed. I was now locked in.

I walked around the shop, my heart thumping with worry, and I knew that I'd be in real trouble if Blaketon discovered my lapse. Sleeping on duty was almost a cardinal sin. I told myself to be calm as I wandered around, seeking a window which might open, or a key which might permit me to leave. But none of the windows was of the opening kind, save for a small one in the toilet, but that wouldn't even admit a cat. And I could not find a key hanging anywhere.

There was only one solution – I'd have to ring the station once more and hope that Sergeant Blaketon was out of the building. I'd ask whoever was on duty to ring Mr Austin again. I'd have to ask him to drive back into town to release me. I had to be out of the shop before six o'clock, otherwise I'd be late for booking off duty, and that would get me into severe trouble . . .

Then it dawned on me that if the station duty constable could ring Mr Austin, why couldn't I? Perhaps I could cover up my crass stupidity! I looked up his number in the directory which lay by the phone, checked my watch and realized he'd almost be back home. I knew he'd be horrified if he was roused again, so I wanted to catch him before he got back into bed. I was aware that he was liable to write a letter of complaint to the Superintendent, but it was a risk I could not avoid.

I rang the number. The telephone rang for a long, long time but eventually a woman sleepily answered.

'Oh,' I said apologetically. 'This is Strensford Police. It's PC Rhea speaking. Is Mr Austin there?'

'No, he's gone to his shop. Your office rang about it.'

'Ah, well, it's urgent. We need to contact him.'

'Well, I'm sorry, but he left well over an hour ago, to lock up his premises, he said. It had been left open.'

'Yes, well, he has locked it, but something urgent has arisen and I thought he might have returned home by now.'

'No, constable, he said it was hardly worth while coming all this way back, so he said he was going fishing off the pier end. He said he'd stay there until it was time to open up at half past eight. He often gets up early to go sea-fishing, constable; he loves every minute of it. That's where you'll find him, sitting on the end of the pier with his fishing rod.'

'Oh, well, I need him urgently but can't reach him . . .'

'What's wrong, officer?' there was alarm in her voice.

I took a deep breath. 'You're going to laugh at this, Mrs Austin, but I'm locked in your shop! I can't get out,' and I explained how this terrible thing had happened.

She burst into laughter and I felt an utter fool. Finally, she said, 'Look, there's no need to worry. Look in Ray's desk, right-hand drawer, in an old toffee box. There's a spare set of keys with a bobbin attached. Use them, and pop them back through the letterbox when you've got out.'

'Thank you!' I breathed. 'Thank you. You don't know how relieved I am!'

'Then come back into the shop one day and tell me. I work there too – there'll be a cup of tea for you, and I know my husband would love to meet you . . .' and she chuckled loudly as she replaced the telephone.

I did find those keys, and I did let myself out, then I tried to resume my patrol as if nothing had happened. But I reckoned the story would surface one day – so I'm telling it now, without exaggeration. I made firm friends of Mr and Mrs Austin, but I often wonder if Sergeant Blaketon ever knew about my lapse.

That morning, as I booked off duty, he asked, with a twinkle in his eye, 'Is everything all right, Rhea?'

'Yes, all correct, sergeant,' I assured him.

2

O well for the sailor lad
That he sings on his boat in the bay.

Alfred Lord Tennyson, 1809–92

To walk the early morning beat in Strensford is an enchanting experience. Such is the appeal of the harbourside and the beach at the dawn of a summer's day that holiday-makers and local residents alike stir themselves from their slumbers and journey to the sea, there to explore the coast and to witness the daily routine of the fishermen. These sturdy, hard-working men may begin their work at any hour of the day or night depending upon the timing of the tides. Sometimes they return to shore in the light of a new dawn, and sometimes they rise even before the sun to busy themselves about their boats or at the nearby fishmarket.

There are times when the undulating waters of the harbour are hidden beneath a floating, constantly moving platform of fishing boats. Men clad in thigh-length waders and thick, dark-blue jerseys known as gansers move from boat to boat with astonishing ease and confidence, while the boats themselves are moored both side by side and stern to prow. They form a solid, gently swaying platform which reaches midway across the water, and from many of them spirals of blue smoke rise from tiny chimneys as their motors idle with a strangely fluid sound. There is the scent too, the distinctive scent of the sea and of fish and fishing, a scent not unpleasant here on the quayside.

In the summer, some of the boats belong to the local

fishermen, but others do come to Strensford as visitors. Some hail from English ports, others come from Scotland, Holland and Scandinavia, but they all seek the shoals of herring which visit Dogger Bank and inhabit the North Sea.

The visitors invariably live upon their boats, sleeping, eating and working within the spotless confines of their accommodation below deck. During their annual visit to Strensford, these ships are a combination of miniature floating homes, factories and fishmarkets. The men on board are dressed for combat both with the sea and with fish, for here you'll find sou'westers, gansers, thigh-length sea-boots and one-piece pale blue denim tops with long sleeves and no buttons.

And always, there is the ever-present scent of fish, the glistening fish scales, the huge boxes of cooling ice and buckets of fresh cleansing water. Cool wetness and fish seem to be inseparable, and in those days boxes of preserving ice were manufactured at local ice factories.

To witness the careful work-a-day preparations by this multinational fleet is fascinating. Daily they brave the wrath of the grey North Sea in boats which seem too small and flimsy when viewed from the staiths but which are sturdy enough to cope with their tough, thankless task.

It is this unique activity which so captivates the holidaymakers, and we policemen who then patrolled the town were privileged to see this routine during our normal duties. And in spite of seeing it time and time again, it never lost its appeal. Sea fishermen live in a self-contained world; it is a unique way of life which is an echo of the past. There was never any overt urgency in their behaviour, just a steady, methodical style born of generations of hard-working men whose chosen career faced nature at its most severe.

Sometimes at night or in the very early dark hours of the morning, that same fleet would position itself far out at sea to undertake its work. From the shore, it could be seen as a distant town of gently moving lights, all arranged in straight lines like formal streets. I've known motorists high on the moors be puzzled by the appearance of the 'mirage' of a new town out in the blackness of the night-time sea, but those are the lights by which these men work to drag from the deep their full nets of struggling fish. And, when the night's work is done, they will return to Strensford to unload and sell their catch, to prepare their boats and equipment for the following day and then to embark once again, depending not upon the passage of time but upon the sequence of high tides and a knowledge of the movements of the herring shoals, or the availability of whiting, cod and other fish.

Although visitors did sometimes join local boats for paid fishing trips, I never anticipated stepping on board any of them, either British or foreign.

But it did happen.

The first time was when I was on early duty, my beat taking me along the harbourside.

My 6.35 a.m. point was at the telephone kiosk in the Fish Market, and on this occasion there was a call for me.

'It's Stan in the office,' said the voice. 'I've a pleasant little job for you.'

'Fire away.' I took my notebook from my tunic pocket and opened its pages on the coinbox so I could write in it.

'It's from a Mrs Maureen McPherson.' He spoke slowly, allowing me time to take down his words. 'From Aberdeen,' and he gave me the address.

'Yes,' I said, having noted those details.

'Her son, Ian, is a crewman on the fishing boat *Waverley* – it's in our harbour all this week. It's registered in Aberdeen, you'll find it easily enough. We've got a request message for him – tell him that his mother rang. It's to say that his wife, Joan, has given birth to a baby boy. She's in the maternity hospital in Aberdeen, and both are doing well. Maybe he'll give his mother a call as soon as possible?'

'I'll be delighted,' I said. The delivery of these so-called 'request messages' was a task we often undertook for those people who did not have a telephone. On this occasion it was a pleasant message, but more often than not we had to deliver news of deaths or severe accidents. News of a happy birth was a very welcome change.

I went cheerfully about my task and soon found the fishing

21

boat. It was moored midway along the harbourside and lay beyond a further three, well into the centre of the full harbour. All seemed at rest, for there was no obvious work going on.

I climbed down to the deck of the nearest boat and by stepping across other decks soon reached the *Waverley*. There was no one on deck, so I tapped on the cabin door, where I was greeted by a thick-set fisherman in the customary heavy navy-blue sweater. In his late forties, he oozed power and authority, a formidable man to cross, I guessed.

'Good morning,' I said as he opened the narrow door.

'Wha' is it?' There was more than a hint of suspicion in his gruff Scots voice. 'It's no' bother, is it?'

'No,' I said. 'It's good news. Is Ian McPherson below?'

'Aye.'

'Could I have a word with him?'

'Here?'

'Yes please.'

'He's busy, doon the galley, but Ah'll fetch him.'

I watched his broad back disappear below and waited until a younger man arrived. He was dark-haired and swarthy, if a little more slender than the previous one. He'd be about twenty-six years old but was almost a carbon-copy of the older man. He was powerful too, thick-set with a strong chin and deep chest. I reckoned he and his father could cope with any kind of 'bother' as they called it.

'Hello,' he said.

'Ian McPherson?'

'Aye, Ah'm Ian, that other was ma dad.'

'Oh, well. It's good news. I've got a message from your mother. It's to say you're a proud dad, Ian. A lovely baby boy, born in Aberdeen maternity hospital. Your wife and baby are both fine. I was asked to inform you. Oh, and you've got to ring your mother.'

His dark eyes misted at my news, and this was followed by the quivering of his bottom lip, both signs of a happy new father. This tough, stolid Scotsman was doing his best not to show any emotion, but he was losing the battle.

'Congratulations,' I said.

'Aye,' he wiped an eye with the rough sleeve of his ganser. 'Look, officer, come along doon. We'll need to celebrate de noo.'

It was rather early in the morning to be drinking, I thought, but I did not like to appear churlish in his moment of happiness, so I followed him downstairs into the tiny, cramped galley. It was spotlessly clean and tidy. I noticed the table was laid for five breakfasts, and as I reached the end of this tiny table, Ian shouted.

'Hey, fellers. Listen to this! Ah'm a dad, a new dad, a little lad, so we've got another crew member, heh?'

Four men rushed in, one of them still in pyjamas, and they slapped him on the back, congratulated him and praised him. Then they turned to the man I'd first met and offered him their congratulations on being a new grandfather. I did likewise.

'Ah've fetched the constable doon for a celebration,' said the new father. 'Set him a place, Donal.'

One of them set a breakfast place at the end of the table and offered me a stool; I sat down, feeling a little bewildered by this turn of events, but Mr McPherson senior said, 'This is a family boat, constable. My lad and oor cousins, that's who we are. It's oors and oors alone. Noo we've a new man to grow in tae the business and tha's good. Verra good. You'll be welcome to celebrate wi' us, seeing t'was you who brought the good news. You'll take breakfast wi' us then?'

'I'll be delighted,' I said, wondering how I'd manage two breakfasts in one short morning. The hotel would have one ready when I returned around nine o'clock.

They busied themselves in the cramped little galley, and then a bottle of Scotch appeared. It was placed in the centre of the table, and six glistening cut glasses were positioned at each of the breakfast settings. Then, as if at some unseen signal, the whole crew of five settled around the table, the pyjama-clad cousin having dressed by this time.

Then Ian's father, whom I took to be the captain of this boat, surprised me by saying, 'Constable, we say grace de noo.'

And they did. Those five hard, rugged Scotsmen bowed their heads as Mr McPherson said grace.

Afterwards he poured a generous tipple of whisky into each glass, and we toasted the health of the new baby and his absent mother. At that, one of them left the table and brought the first course of the breakfast. It was porridge, unsweetened, thick and eaten with salt.

I stayed there too long; I drank a little too much of their whisky and ate far too much of their plain but wholesome breakfast, but I was pleased I'd eaten a Scots breakfast on board an immaculate fishing boat with such a caring family.

But the most memorable sight was of those five tough seamen with bowed heads meekly saying grace before they ate.

Another opportunity to go aboard a boat occurred when the daughter of the proprietor of our digs, the Breckdale Private Hotel, asked if I could obtain a clog for her. Anne, tall, pretty and blonde, asked me at lunchtime one day.

'A clog?' I must have sounded surprised.

'Yes, a real clog, a Dutchman's clog, one of those wooden ones. I'd love one of those.'

'Why do you want a clog?' I asked.

'To bring good look,' she answered. 'A real clog, as worn by a Dutch person, brings good luck.'

I never heard of this superstition. I knew that fisherfolk the world over were highly superstitious – the local ones, for example, believed that if the family kept a black cat, it would ensure the safe return from sea of the man-of-the-house. But once at sea, the word 'cat' had never to be mentioned because it would bring ill fortune, although some felt it sensible to keep a black cat on board. In the event of a shipwreck, this was first to be rescued.

Other forbidden words included *drowning, witch, death, pig, dog, rabbit* and *rat*, as well as references to clergymen and words for various parts of the human body!

If, on their way to their boat, the fishermen met either a cross-eyed person, a woman wearing a white apron, a clergyman or a hare, there was nothing that could be done to avert a sea-faring disaster other than to turn around and go home. There is still a belief that sea-birds contain the souls of the drowned and that their cries are the cries of the dead who are warning the living against the storms and hidden dangers.

But I knew nothing about clogs bringing good luck. A similar superstition was that if a person carried a fisherman's sea-boots to him, they should always be borne under the arm and not over the shoulder, for fear of bringing bad luck. Another belief in some places was that old shoes should be thrown after boats as they left port as a means of either bringing good fortune or, I suggest, getting rid of old shoes!

So far as I know, Dutchmen's clogs did not enter this little world of ancient beliefs, but because of Anne's sincere request I promised to do my best to acquire one for her. So, whenever I worked a harbourside beat, I examined from a distance the decks of the Dutch fleet, albeit never really expecting to see a discarded clog.

But one morning, about 6.15 a.m., I espied the very thing. It was a large, yellow-painted clog made of wood, with the familiar upturned toe, and it looked exactly right for Anne. It looked huge from where I was standing on the staith, but it was lying on the prow of a Dutch fishing boat, resting on a pile of coiled rope as the fishermen busied themselves in preparation for sailing.

My heart leapt at the sight. I'd never really expected to find Anne's treasure, but there it was, and it looked like a cast-off because it had a hole in the sole. The hole was about the size of half-crown, well over an inch across, and I wondered if clogs were re-soled like shoes. If so, how was it done? Then I wondered if it was a true cast-off or whether it was there to be thrown for good luck, after some departing vessel in times to come? Or perhaps it would be thrown overboard as rubbish?

But I could not let this opportunity pass without making some effort to obtain that clog, even if it meant buying it as a present. The first problem was how to gain legitimate possession of it.

Possession would then present the second problem, i.e. how to convey it back to Anne via the police station while I was dressed in full police uniform. This was even more of a problem because the eagle-eyed Sergeant Blaketon was on duty this morning.

But first things first. I would make an effort to get my hands on that clog. I knew the boat was preparing to sail so I dared not wait until the end of my first period of patrolling, and I was due back at the police station at 9 a.m. to report 'off duty' for my refreshment break. I had to get that clog immediately so I could hand it to Anne when I arrived at the hotel for breakfast. I stared at it for a long time as I debated the best course of action. I know that my mesmeric stance caused many early-strolling visitors to peer over the harbour rails, probably wondering why the constabulary was paying so much attention to a Dutch fishing boat.

In the midst of my thoughts, a man emerged from the cabin. He noticed me, and I waved my hands to indicate that I wished to speak with him, but he just waved back and went about his work. I decided I must be bold so I descended the steep stone steps which led down the side of the harbour wall to the level of the boats. I crossed one or two swaying decks before I arrived at the Dutch boat. The man was busy with some fishing nets.

'Good morning,' I said, realizing I was speaking loudly as one tends to do when addressing foreigners.

'Gut mornen,' I think he replied, but I could see the worried look on his face.

It was then that I realized that in other countries the relationship between the police and the public wasn't quite the same as that which existed between the British bobby and his public. By arriving on his boat without permission, I had probably put the fear of God into this poor fellow. He probably thought I was going to impound his vessel, arrest his crew or arrange a Customs search.

'Do you speak English?' I asked.

He shook his head and continued to wear a very harassed expression. The last thing I wanted was to frighten him, and it did cross my mind that, if I antagonized him too greatly, I might have to swim back to the police station.

'Does anyone on board speak English?' I tried.

He raised a finger as if in understanding and disappeared below; I could hear a jabbering of tongues and then five men emerged. My heart sank into my boots. I'd done it now . . . I had no chance against five powerful Dutchmen.

'Good morning.' I tried the Englishman's traditional approach, the one which seems to be used in any situation.

It brought no reply. They stood and stared at me in the way that cows stand and stare at those who picnic in their fields.

I was almost surrounded by these burly, tough fishermen. I decided that perhaps Anne did not really need a clog after all.

'Does anyone speak English?' I spoke slowly now, if a little too loudly, my voice rising in pitch as if to betray my fears.

'*Ja*,' said one of them after a long pause. 'I spik Inglish.'

'Ah,' I breathed a sigh of relief. Now for my strange proposition.

'My-girl-friend,' I said slowly, thinking the true relationship would be too difficult to explain. 'She-wants-a-clog-to-keep-for-good-luck,' and I pointed to the clog I'd earmarked.

'Clog?' asked the English-speaker.

I smiled and nodded furiously, then continued very slowly. 'Yes, she-believes-that-a-clog-like-that-brings-good-fortune-to-her. She-has-asked-me-to-find-a-clog-for-her. I-saw-that-clog-and-thought-it-might-not-be-wanted . . .'

'Ah!' beamed the English-speaking fellow. 'I understand. She likes charm, hey? A charm? The clog, it will be a charm for her? For luck? She want this charm?'

'*Ja*,' I tried, and once more nodded furiously, hoping the reason for my presence would be fully understood.

Now they were all smiling and laughing, and I sensed a deep feeling of relief among them.

'Yes,' said the English-speaker. 'Yes, she can have the clog.'

He gabbled something at the others in his own tongue, and they all smiled and laughed, and I knew how they felt. Relief swept across them and, I must admit, across me.

'Come,' said my new friend. 'Down below, with us. For breakfast? I will get you the clog now.'

And so I joined them all below deck, where I enjoyed a large mug of coffee in their spotless galley. They presented me with the worn-out clog, and once they discovered I was friendly, I found out they could all speak a smattering of English.

Soon afterwards, I left with the huge clog. It must have been size 12, and I now had the problem of hiding it for the next couple of hours or so, as I smuggled it back to Anne via the police station. I couldn't take it directly to her because the hotel was a long way off my present beat, and to be found absent from one's beat was to risk a disciplinary charge, especially with Sergeant Blaketon on duty.

My cape provided the answer. When on patrol, even on summer days, we carried our voluminous capes by folding them flat into several folds and then slinging them over our shoulders. They were ideal waterproof garments, and when worn about our bodies, they also concealed a great deal. I've known policemen do their wives' shopping at times, and then smuggle it home beneath their flowing capes; they can hide fish-and-chips at supper time, Christmas presents at Christmas time, and I once knew a constable who smuggled a custard pie home beneath his cape. So, by draping my cape around my shoulders, I would be able to conceal the large, wooden clog from prying eyes.

Although it wasn't raining and although it wasn't particularly chilly that morning, I completed the remainder of the first half of my patrol with my cape concealing the clog. I carried the clog in one hand, with my thumb tucked beneath the button of my breast pocket for support, and none of the passing citizens seemed to think it odd that I should be dressed for rain.

I entered the police station to book off and decided I would make a quick dash to the counter and poke my head through the enquiry hatch without entering the office. I would call, 'PC Rhea, booking off, refreshment break,' and then vanish before anyone could forestall my dash from the building or ask silly questions.

But I hadn't bargained for Sergeant Blaketon.

He saw me before I saw him, and called out, 'Rhea, just a minute!'

My heart sank. Now I had to enter the office, and there he was, with his back to the fireplace, beaming almost villainously as I walked in. The office man, a senior constable called Stan who was local to Strensford, was seated on a tall stool at the counter, and he flashed me a brief but sympathetic smile.

'Ah, Rhea,' Sergeant Blaketon said. 'Anything to report from No. 1 Beat this morning?'

'No, sergeant,' I smiled. 'All correct. I'm just heading for breakfast.'

'No trouble on the Dutch fishing boats then?'

'Trouble, sergeant?' I wondered how much he knew, or how much he had seen. I had not noticed him on the quayside.

'Trouble, Rhea. Bother. Mayhem. That sort of thing, the sort of thing that might require the presence of a constable. Nothing like that, was there? Nothing to report?'

The crafty character must have seen me on the deck of that boat, or else he'd been talking to someone else who had seen me. I thought I'd string him along to see what he was aiming at.

'No, sergeant,' I decided that brief answers were the best.

'Oh, I just wondered, I heard that a young constable had been seen on board a Dutch fishing boat this morning. That's your beat, so I wondered if it might have been trouble of some kind.'

'No, sergeant,' I said, and I knew I was blushing by this time. 'No trouble.'

'It was you, though, was it, Rhea?' he persisted.

'I did go on board for a chat, sergeant, just a friendly chat. Passing the time of day, you know.'

'Ah!' he beamed. 'So my information was correct. But there was no trouble, no complaints, no problems?'

'None at all, sergeant.'

'Hmm. Well, that's all right then. So long as there is no trouble. So you'll be off for your breakfast then?'

'Yes, sergeant, I must be off. The hotel likes us to be on time . . .'

'Not raining on your beat, was it? Or cold?'

I thought fast. He was moving to the subject of my cape now, so I smiled and said, 'It was a bit chilly, sergeant, a breeze off the sea, you know. It can blow a bit chilly on the harbourside at dawn.'

'Yes, so it can,' he paused, and at that precise moment the telephone rang. The office constable answered it and said, 'Sergeant, it's for you. The Superintendent.'

As he moved to take the call, Sergeant Blaketon looked at me as if he was going to say something, but already I was moving towards the door. I bolted out of the office and was hurrying towards the exit of the police station as I heard Sergeant Blaketon in an animated conversation with the Superintendent. I'd been saved literally in the nick of time.

But before I reached the door, a voice halted me. It was Stan, the PC on office duty.

'Outside, quick,' he said as he bustled me out of the station.

'What's the matter, Stan?' I almost shouted.

'Have you got a bloody clog off that boat?' he asked me, eyeing the bulky shape beneath my cape.

'Yes,' I said. 'Why? It was given to me.'

He laughed. 'Then get to hell out of here, and quick! He was after it, he wanted it, that bloody sergeant you've brought over from Ashfordly. He noticed it there last night but there was no one about to ask, so he was going to have a word with the skipper this morning. It seems his wife has always wanted a genuine Dutch clog to put on her mantelpiece, but I can't think why . . . Anyway, it had gone by the time he got down to the harbourside this morning . . .'

'I'm going!' I said, and I almost ran to the hotel. Anne was delighted, and I got a double helping of sausages that morning.

The next time I boarded a fishing vessel occurred after a spate of shop-breakings in Strensford. In those days, the crime of breaking into shop premises to steal goods was popularly known as shop-breaking, but since 1968 all such 'break and entry' offences have been grouped together under the single heading of *burglary*.

Whenever we paraded for a night shift during that short sojourn at the seaside, we were reminded that someone, probably a lone operator, was breaking into shops all over the town. The stolen property was not particularly valuable. like cameras or radio sets, nor was it particularly useful, like food or clothing. Most of the attacked premises were the tourist-souvenir type of shop, selling cheap oddments such as jewellery, watches, ornaments and knick-knacks of the kind no truly discerning visitor would take home. They were all close to the harbourside too.

On one occasion, for example, three flying ducks in plaster were taken, and we did wonder if the thief ran a boarding house. Almost all the boarding houses in Strensford at that time had plaster ducks flying up their walls, and some had gnomes in their gardens.

The CID reckoned the breaker was a youth, perhaps a visitor to one of the holiday camps or caravan sites, but whoever he was, he always escaped. Their reckoning was based partly on the fact that he must be slim and agile to be able to wriggle through some of the skylights which were his chief source of entry, and another part of their logic was that the mediocre stuff he stole would hardly appeal to an adult. It would certainly not appeal to a handler of stolen goods or an antique-dealer.

Throughout those warm summer nights, therefore, the uniform branch maintained observations upon the streets, but we never caught our man.

More shops were raided, more junk was stolen and eventually the Chamber of Trade, and the *Strensford Times,* began to ask what the police were doing about the sudden and unwarranted major crime wave. The local Superintendent had the sense to issue a statement to the paper: 'We are maintaining observations and are utilizing all available manpower in an attempt to curb this seasonal outbreak of crime. We believe it is the work of visiting criminals.'

This series of shopbreakings occurred long before the days of collators who assembled and disseminated crime-beating information, and long before the police had computers, which could assess crime intelligence. As I read the Occurrence Book each day, however, I did become aware that the shops were raided on the same nights that we received calls from some sleepy residents that a horse was loose and roaming the streets. It had been heard several times in the dead of night, but no one had actually seen the horse. There developed a theory that the shop-breaker was a horseman and that he carefully studied the movements of the police before committing his crimes.

In an attempt to gain more information, I took several Occurrence Books, which were logs of all daily events, and checked them meticulously for (a) calls about horses loose at night in Strensford and (b) shop-breakings which occurred around the same time. And a pattern did emerge. The breaks were occurring around two o'clock in the morning, the very time the policemen went into the station for their mid-shift break – this made it seem they *were* being observed. Furthermore, all the occasions when the horse had been reported were around the same mid-shift time.

Then, by one of those strokes of fortune by which great crimes are solved, I had to compile a list of the times of high tides for the information of Force Headquarters – someone over there was compiling a Spring Tide Early Warning System. As I listed the times known to Strensford, I suddenly wondered whether the raids could be linked with tidal times. I was really thinking of the swing bridge across the harbour which opened at times of high tide; high tides occurred twice a day, with about twelve hours between each high water. I did wonder if our horse-riding villain came across that bridge into town, so I carried out my survey over several months.

To cut a long story short, I did not voice my opinions to anyone else but decided to carry out a spell of observations whenever my night duty coincided with a high tide which occurred around 2 a.m. The tide was almost full for some time both before and after the official high-tide time; this meant there was often full water while the policemen were having their mid-shift meals . . . and that meant the fishing boats were under preparation for sailing. My mind was working fast.

'Sergeant,' I spoke to Sergeant Blaketon at the beginning of one night shift. 'Can I work a harbourside beat tonight but take my break later than normal, say 3 a.m.?'

'Why, Rhea? What are you scheming now?'

I was in two minds not to tell him, but I felt he would not grant this odd request without knowing the story, and so, in the peace of the sergeant's office, I explained. To give him credit, he did listen.

'Right,' he said. 'Do it. And I'll be there too. We'll see this out together, Rhea. We'll show these townies that us country coppers can arrest their shop-breakers!'

We arranged to meet at 1.45 a.m., and together we would seek a place of concealment from where we could overlook the swing bridge, the harbourside and quays, the herring boats and the main thoroughfares into town.

That night, high tide was at 2.33 a.m., and as we watched from an alley overlooking the harbour, we could see the lights of the boats as their crews were preparing to sail to the herring grounds. And then we saw him.

A tall, lithe young man left the shadows of the harbourside and made his noisy way into town. A Dutchman, in clogs. Clip-clopping into town.

'There's the horse, sergeant!' I hissed at him.

'Where, Rhea?'

'The clogs!' I snapped. 'They sound like a horse walking at night, when the streets are empty. This is our breaker, a Dutch seaman!'

'Right, we need to catch him with the evidence. Wait here until he comes back with his loot.'

That was true. We had no evidence yet, certainly not enough to convict him, and so we simply waited and then, some forty minutes later, we heard the clip-clop of his return journey.

'Nice work, Rhea,' beamed Sergeant Blaketon. 'You'll get high praise for this one. Now, when he's past us on the way to his ship, we go and get him. Get him *before* he gets back to his boat – I'm not sure what the law is about arresting foreign nationals on board their own ships. But the arrest is yours, so do it on British soil.'

But as the tall, young Dutchman passed us with a carrier bag full of his ill-gotten gains, he heard our movements. He started to run. Even in those clumsy clogs, he covered the ground at a remarkable speed, and he sounded like a horse at full gallop. I was sure we'd get more complaints about galloping horses, but right now Blaketon and I were hard on his heels.

The Dutchman beat us to his ship. He slithered down a harbourside ladder and reached his boat as we reached the harbour's edge. Then, before our very eyes, he threw the offending bag into the harbour, where it sank immediately.

'Our bloody evidence!' snapped Sergeant Blaketon.

But the youth was doing something even worse. As Sergeant Blaketon stood and watched, he removed both his clogs and threw them one by one over the side of the boat. Each landed with a splash. One filled with water and sank, while the other sailed away into the darkness.

'He's thrown his clogs away!' gasped Sergeant Blaketon.

I felt very sorry for poor Oscar Blaketon at that point, for we could not prove our case. But I do know that someone from CID had a word with the captain, and all the shops, save the final one, had their goods returned. The sixteen-year-old boy was a kleptomaniac. There was no prosecution because of international complications but the shop-breakings did come to an end. And so did reports of horses galloping through Strensford at night.

But Sergeant Blaketon still hasn't obtained a real Dutch clog for his mantelpiece.

3

He that is robbed not wanting what is stolen,
Let him not know it, and he's not robb'd at all.
William Shakespeare, 1564–1616

When patrolling the quiet streets of Strensford during those
warm summer nights, my mind turned frequently to the initial
police training course I had undergone. I recalled the essence of
lectures about all manner of fascinating things, and one of the
subjects was crime. It was a subject which intrigued all the
students, and some went on to become clever detectives.

One aspect of crime which was discussed at length was that
which is known in Latin as *mens rea*. It is a curious phrase which
refers to the state of mind of a criminal, his criminal intent in
other words. It is that guilty or blameworthy state of mind
during which crimes are committed. During our lectures, we
were given questions which endeavoured to show us the
difference between an *intent* and an *attempt* to commit crime.
We were told that a person's criminal intent was rarely punish-
able – a man can intend to commit burglary, rape or murder,
but the mere intention to do such a thing, however serious, is
not in itself a crime. On the other hand, an attempt to commit a
crime is illegal.

We wondered if a person could be guilty of an attempted
larceny when it was impossible to commit the full crime. One
example of this is a pickpocket who dips his hand into a man's
pocket to steal a wallet, but the pocket is empty. Thus he cannot
complete his intended crime. So is he guilty of attempted

larceny? If the pocket had contained a wallet, then most certainly the attempt could be completed, if not the full crime . . .

Many academic questions of this kind were discussed, and it is fair to say that few of us ever dreamed we would be confronted with real examples of this kind of legal puzzle. In the world of practical policing, crimes were committed, criminals were arrested and proceedings were taken. The academic side of things was left to the lawyers.

At least that's what I thought until I came across Hedda Flynn.

Although my time in Strensford was short and somewhat fragmented, due to the shifts I worked, I did begin to recognize those whom I saw regularly. In the main, they were local people going about their business or pleasure in their small and charming town. Hedda Flynn was such a person. He caught my attention when I noticed he was beginning to loiter around the entrance to St Patrick's Roman Catholic Church and that he chose to do so at a time the local churches were experiencing a spate of offertory box thefts.

Several boxes had been broken into during the early summer months, the technique being by the simple medium of using what police described as a 'blunt instrument' to force open the lids. This was probably a screwdriver. The cash contents, the amount of which was invariably unknown, were stolen. Although these crimes were comparatively minor, they did present problems.

No community, whether in a town or a village, likes its church to be attacked in any way, and these crimes were considered very distasteful. It was felt they were the work of a travelling vagrant, because none of the boxes contained a large amount. The task of forcing the wooden lids and removing the contents would often result in the theft of only a few shillings, hardly a major crime.

Some good Christians argued that if the thief was so poor that the funds within the offertory boxes were vital to his existence, why not let him take them? After all, wasn't the Church there to provide for the poor? If the fellow had asked the priest or vicar for some money, it would probably have been given. This was an argument which did not impress the police. In their books a crime was a crime, whatever the reason for its commission.

As a form of crime prevention, we toured all the churches and chapels within our Division and suggested to their priests, vicars and ministers that they make their offertory boxes more substantial and secure. We even suggested they enclose them within the walls of their churches or make them of metal, then cement them into the floor. Some did this.

One who did not follow our advice was Monsignor Joseph O'Flaherty of St Patrick's Roman Catholic Church, and it was his offertory box which I suspected was an object of great interest to Hedda Flynn.

There was a time when I considered arresting Hedda under the Vagrancy Act of 1824, for that quaint old statute created an offence of being a suspected person or reputed thief loitering with intent to commit a crime. Certainly, Hedda had undertaken a good deal of loitering, usually around lunch-time, but his intentions were unknown. There was no evidence that he intended to commit a crime, nor could he be described as either a suspected person or a reputed thief. The law lays down quite specifically what is meant by 'suspected person', and Hedda's behaviour had not quite lifted him into that category. In fact, he was a very decent fellow.

Having noticed him once or twice, I carried out my own discreet enquiries and learned he was a married man with two small children. He worked behind the counter of a gentlemen's clothes shop in Strensford for what was probably a pittance, and he would be about thirty-five years old. He was a small, dark man whose own clothes hung from him; they appeared to be several sizes too large, and I guessed that, as a child, his mother had always bought him clothes which were too large, so that he could grow into them. I reckoned he never had grown into them but that he still hoped he would.

His thin, sallow face with its bushy eyebrows and dark troubled eyes gave him the appearance of a haunted man, and it was clear something was troubling him. Was he a lapsed Catholic who wanted to return to the faith?

On the other hand, I wondered if his conscience was troubling him. I wondered if he was fiddling the till at work, or whether he had another woman in tow, or, of course, whether he was the offertory box thief who was plaguing the district.

I decided to speak to Monsignor O'Flaherty about Hedda and about the risks to his offertory box. I had seen the box in question – it was a simple wooden container screwed to a table at the back of the church, and it would be a simple matter to force the lid with a screwdriver and remove its meagre contents.

I knocked on the door of the presbytery and was admitted by the priest's housekeeper, who showed me to a study littered with books and watercolours. Some stood on the floor and others filled every possible space on the wall. I waited, intrigued by the smell of the place and its wonderful array of books and paintings.

The Monsignor came in, smiling and happy. He was dressed in a clerical grey suit with a carnation in his buttonhole. He was a very rounded man with a rosy red face and thinning grey hair above very bright and twinkling blue eyes. He looked like a man who enjoyed life.

'Ah!' he smiled. ''Tis the law. You'll be having a drink then?'?'

'Good morning, Monsignor,' I said. 'I'd like a coffee please.'

'Coffee, is it? I was thinking of something more congenial, like a dram of the morning dew? So is it coffee or whisky, or perhaps both?'

'Just coffee, Monsignor. I'm on duty.'

'So it's official, then? You're not coming to see me about your spiritual welfare or to get married or something? Haven't I seen you at Mass?'

'Yes, but this is police work.'

'Then sit yourself down, son, and I'll arrange the coffee. Sugar? Milk?'

I requested both, and the tray soon appeared with coffee for us both and a glass of his 'wee dram'. While we drank them, he learned my name and something of my own family background. The introductions and pleasantries over, we turned to the purpose of my visit.

I began with the attacks on offertory boxes and put forward various suggestions for making them less vulnerable to thieves. He listened attentively and said he had seen reports in the *Strensford Gazette* about the other attacks.

'But, you see, I always make sure there is a collection plate on the table at the back of the church, close to the door. And in that plate, there is always a few coins; either the faithful put them there or I do, so if a thief does come, he'll grab that money and he'll leave the box alone. Now, I don't mind him taking those loose coins, and indeed, I'll seldom know whether he has or not, will I? It's only copper, but it could be food for a starving man. And our offertory box has never been forced open.'

I admired the sheer logic of this and now recalled the large wooden collection plate which was always on the table near the main door. It often had a half crown or a florin in it, with an assortment of smaller coins, such as a sixpence and one or two pennies.

'There is something else, Monsignor.' I emptied my coffee cup and he refilled it from the percolator.

'Go on.'

I told him about Hedda Flynn and my suspicions. He listened and then smiled in understanding.

'Hedda is a good man,' he said. 'A very good man, a faithful member of my congregation and as honest as the day is long. He would never do anything wrong to anyone, let alone steal from the Church.'

'He does linger about the back of the church.' I had come across this very Christian attitude many times before but police officers are cynical and distrustful. 'I feel I ought to warn you of his activities.'

'Thanks anyway, constable, but I know Hedda. And I might add, I know his wife too. Now there's a holy woman. Mass at half-seven every morning. Benediction twice a week. Generous to the church, generous to a fault she is. Wonderful wife for Hedda, wonderful mother for her family. A church helper, too. She does the flowers for the altar, cleans the church – she's a saint, constable, a true saint. Hedda is a very lucky man, very lucky.'

I felt I had fulfilled my purpose. I had drawn his attention to the risks and I had even named a suspect. Perhaps I had been wrong to do the latter, for it was clear that the Monsignor thought a lot about the Flynn family, although I did wonder why, if Hedda was such a good Catholic, he hung around the back of the church at lunch-time rather than enter to kneel and pray. But it was time to go.

Before I left, Monsignor O'Flaherty showed me some of his books and explained that he collected watercolours by the local artist Scott Hodgson, hence his massive assortment of his, and other artists', works.

Within a week, two more offertory boxes had been broken into, each in parish churches in nearby moorland villages, and even I felt that Hedda could not be responsible for those crimes. He didn't have a car, and I knew he had been at work during the material times. But he continued to hang around the back of St Patrick's . . .

Then came the day I decided to do something positive. It happened because late one Friday afternoon I chanced to be walking past the main door of the church, in full uniform, just as the small, untidy figure of Hedda was vanishing inside. He had not seen me, and so I crossed the street and climbed the wide and steep flight of steps up to the entrance.

I must admit that my heart was beating; I wondered if I was about to arrest a thief actually in the act of committing his crime and found myself tiptoeing across the threshold and into the interior of the large building with its subdued lighting and hushed atmosphere. I had to find out what he was up to.

The large, ribbed door was open, as it always was during the daytime hours, and I sneaked inside. I removed my uniform cap and found myself in the shadows of the rearmost part of the church, my soft-soled boots making no sound on the marble floor. And I could see Hedda at the table which bore the offertory box. He stood with his head bowed in the silence of the empty church. The box had not been touched, but he was gazing down upon it, both hands resting on the table.

I did not know what to do. He had committed no crime, not yet. I waited. He stood there, almost as if in prayer, and then turned to leave. He moved quickly, almost abruptly, and suddenly found himself face to face with me, my uniform buttons catching the multi-coloured lights of the stained glass windows.

'Oh, Holy Mother of God, you gave me a fright, so you did, standing there like that,' he said.

'What are you doing, Mr Flynn?' I asked.

'Doing, officer? Nothing. I came to say a prayer or two, that's all. Why should that interest the police?' There was bravado in his voice, but I could hear the tremors as he spoke.

'Mr Flynn. We have been having a lot of cash stolen from offertory boxes in recent weeks. We're keeping our eyes open for the thief . . .'

'My God, you don't think I'm the thief! Oh, Jesus, now that is terrible. Really terrible . . . No, I'm no thief, sir, never in a million years. I mean, look, the box has not been touched . . .'

'Then what were you doing?' I had to press home my questions now. 'If you were praying, why weren't you kneeling in one of the pews?'

He hung his head, and I saw tears in his eyes.

His small, drawn face had a haunted look, a desperate look which I could see clearly now that I was so close to him. It did not take a clever person to realize that he was sorely troubled in some way. I still wondered if he had intended to break into the offertory box and whether his strong faith, coupled with the atmosphere of the church surroundings, had defeated him.

'I need to talk to someone,' he said, looking around, but we were alone in the vast emptiness of the church. 'I wanted to talk to Monsignor but he thinks such a lot of Teresa.'

'Teresa?' I asked, hoping my voice sounded gentle and encouraging.

'My wife,' he said, wiping his eyes roughly with his sleeve. 'She's a . . . well, they say she's a good, holy woman, you see, but . . .'

'Go on,' I spoke softly now, cognizant of the atmosphere in which we stood and increasingly aware that he was about to unburden himself of a massive problem of some kind. And now

I was sure he was no thief.

'Well, you're a Catholic. I've seen you at Mass,' he said. 'So that makes it easier, you'll understand what I'm saying. I must talk to someone, I'm getting desperate . . .'

I wondered about moving outside but realized the church probably provided the best surroundings for whatever he wished to say. I smiled at him and said, 'Well, Mr Flynn, here I am, and I am very happy to listen to you.'

He told me that he received £15.17s.6d weekly as wages from his work at the clothes shop, with an annual bonus paid at Christmas which came to around £30. He said it was just enough to live on – he could not afford luxuries or holidays, but because he could buy his clothes at reduced prices, he could manage to support his wife and his family.

'But, you see, constable, I give Teresa all my wages, except for the 17s.6d. I keep that for myself – I like an occasional drink, and sometimes I take her to the pictures. She gets the £15, and we use the bonus for Christmas presents.'

'Go on,' I said.

'Well, as I said, she is a good Catholic woman, a very good one. In fact she's besotted with her religion. It's become a mania . . .'

'How do you mean? A mania?'

'Well, I give her my wages and I've found out she's not been paying the household bills – you know, food, rent, rates, heating, that sort of thing. I've discovered that for nearly three months now she's not paid anyone. I've had the grocer on to me – that's how I found out, and she's run a big bill up at the Co-Op. The Electricity Board is shouting for payment, and others too.'

'So what's she been doing with the money?'

'She's donated it all to the church, constable. Here, to this church. I found out that she comes on a Friday afternoon, straight after I've given her the money over lunch, and she's been putting it all into this offertory box. All the housekeeping. £15! Damn it, it's hard enough to find five bob every week for the collection, but to give the lot, my entire income . . .'

'You've mentioned it to her?'

'Yes, of course,' tears were streaming down his face now.

'And what does she say?' I asked.

'She says the Lord will provide.'

'Can't you explain that the system doesn't work like that? Surely she knows you must give according to your means, not give all your income!'

'I've tried, so Lord help me, I've tried. But it's no good, she's gone off her head, to be sure. I've tried keeping some money back, she accuses me of failing in my duty as a husband and she demands the correct amount of housekeeping. I've always given her it, always, with never a quibble and no trouble till now. I mean, am I within my rights to withhold the housekeeping from her?'

'She must have something to spend on the family,' I said. 'But you could pay the grocery bills and so on.'

'She insists that I give her the money, but whatever I give her, she pushes into this box and says the Lord will provide! She has absolute faith in her religion, and cannot see doubt anywhere. She maintains that if we provide the church with money, the Lord will provide us with all we need. I can get no sense out of her.'

'I think a word with the Monsignor is called for,' I decided.

'He thinks she is wonderful, such a supporter of his church. I don't think he'll understand.'

'He will if he knows the truth. I think he'll listen to me,' I said with confidence. 'Come on, we'll both go.'

He followed me like a small dog, and I could well see him being dominated by his fanatical wife. We arrived at the presbytery, where the round and happy priest greeted us both, albeit with some surprise on his face due to memories of our recent and previous meeting, and my earlier suspicions of Hedda Flynn.

We had a cup of tea because it was the Monsignor's tea-time, and he listened to me while pursing his lips and looking solemnly at Hedda Flynn. When I'd finished, Monsignor addressed the worried Hedda.

'Is this all true then, Hedda my boy?'

'Yes, Monsignor,' he said. 'The constable thought it best if I came to you, although the Lord knows what we can do about her.'

'She's smitten with the faith, so she is,' smiled the priest. 'And terrible it is when folks get like that. Now, if we – or if I – tell her she's doing wrong, that she's sinning even or mis-behaving in the sight of God, she might go all to pieces, eh? We might lose her all together. She won't understand at all. If she's so smitten, we'd by playing with dangerous emotions, so I think we'll leave her to her own devices – but we'll be cunning with it,' he added with a smile.

'But Monsignor,' I protested on behalf of Hedda Flynn. 'You can't let her go on giving *all* the family income to the church . . .'

His eyes flashed, albeit with understanding. 'I can, constable, I can, and I will. But I can give it all back to Hedda, not to Teresa.'

He stood up and went to a safe behind a painting on the wall, unlocked it and handed a roll of notes to Hedda.

'Here you are, Hedda Flynn. I'd been wondering where these huge amounts were coming from, and one day I saw Teresa stuffing the money into the box. I didn't think she could afford all this but didn't like to offend her or you by questioning your generosity. Now I know the truth, and it's your money. So take it. And now, you must continue to let her think she's doing the right thing – it'll keep the peace at home, eh? Let her put the money into the box, and then, every Friday, you come around at tea-time, and I'll give it back to you. How's that?'

'Oh, thank you, Father. Thank you,' beamed the happy fellow. 'Now I can pay all my bills . . . yes, I'll do what you say. But isn't that being deceitful? Isn't it unfair to Teresa to deceive her in this way?'

'I think the constable will agree I'm committing no crime by breaking into my own offertory box to give you your own money back. So just tell your Teresa that the Lord is providing as she believes He will, and let it rest there,' suggested the Monsignor. 'Don't try to explain. Let this thing work itself out.'

And I agreed. I was pleased Hedda wasn't the thief, and later I saw Teresa walking with a saintly air about her, believing the Lord was providing all her family needs.

We never did catch the other person who was raiding the offertory boxes. I can only hope it was someone whose need was as genuine and as great as that of Hedda Flynn.

Another man with a theft problem was Rugby-player Ted Donaldson, a strapping local butcher who stood six foot six inches tall and who weighed seventeen stone. His worry caused my mind to return to my training school lectures and to problems of criminal intent, or *mens rea* as legal men prefer to call it.

'Gotta minute, officer?' he approached me as I stood beside the telephone kiosk in Strensford's bustling fishmarket.

'Yes,' I said, wondering why this massive fellow wore such a worried look.

'You might have to arrest me,' he said, and I must admit it was a thought that did not appeal to me, even if he was currently very docile and submissive.

'Why, have you done something wrong?' I asked.

'Dunno,' he said, and with that he produced a brown leather wallet from his jacket pocket. It was the type many men carried, the sort which could be bought at most chain stores. Then he produced another identical one and showed me them both, weighing one in each of his massive hands.

'Identical, aren't they?' he said, and I nodded.

'So, what's the problem?' I put to him.

'You've not had a report of a robbery with violence, have you?' he asked. 'You chaps are not looking for a bloke like me?'

'No,' I said. 'Should we be looking for somebody like you?'

'Bloody funny,' he said. 'Well, I'd better tell you the story.'

He reminded me that the summer season in Strensford could attract some unsavoury characters, and in recent summers there had been a spate of hit-and-run pickpockets, handbag snatches and portable radio thefts. Teams of thieves would operate together, preying on wandering folks when they least expected it. Their technique was simple. In the crowds of a busy holiday resort, they would jostle a holiday-maker, and in the ensuing bustle and uncertainty they would relieve a man of his wallet, a woman of her handbag or a youngster of anything he or she carried – portable radios and cameras were popular targets. It was with such crimes in mind that uniformed police officers patrolled the crowded areas.

'Well,' said Ted. 'I'm a big bloke but two or three of 'em could have a go at me. Anyway, yesterday, I had some money to pay a bill for my father. Cash it was. I had £150 in my wallet and was aware of those villains. I reckoned they wouldn't really have a go at me . . . but, well . . .'

He paused. 'They did?'

'I thought they did,' he said, licking his lips.

'Thought? What do you mean?'

'Well, there was I, minding my own business and walking through the crowds along by the Amusements, when these two slobs knocked into me and nearly bowled me over. Running like hell, they were. Well, I nearly fell or tripped or something. Anyway, the minute I got my balance, I felt my pocket – and my wallet had gone.'

'And you're a Rugby player of some note in this town?' I could visualize the following sequence of events.

'Yeh, well, I'm not one for letting things like that go unchallenged, in a manner of speaking. So I set off after them and caught the one who'd knocked me.'

'And?'

'Well, there was a lot of hassle and shouting when I brought him down – with a good tackle, mind – and I shouted something like "My wallet!" I shouted a lot more besides I might add, so he might not have heard everything clearly . . . Well, he stuttered and stammered and gave me this.' He showed me one of the brown wallets. 'Then, like a bloody snake, he wriggled free and was off. Like lightning, he was. He vanished into the crowd.'

'But you'd got your wallet back?'

'No,' he said. 'That's the problem. When I opened this one, I found it had no money inside and thought they'd cleaned me out. They'd been quick, I thought, but when I got home my own wallet was on my dressing-table.'

'Full of money?'

'Full of money,' he said, licking his lips again. 'So this one wasn't mine. It looks like mine, but well, I didn't look at it closely at that time, what with all the hassle. So those lads hadn't robbed me. They'd just been a bit rough and careless as they ran through the crowd.'

'So you've robbed that youth of his wallet?' I said.

'Yes, I have, haven't I?' and he passed the slim, empty wallet over to me.

My mind was now racing over those training lectures, struggling with the intricacies of *mens rea* and wondering whether this qualified as a confession to a crime.

But was it a crime?

I opened the wallet and looked through its meagre contents. There was no name or address inside, although I did find a £1 note tucked deep into one of its folds, and some small, square snapshots of a pretty teenaged girl. But nothing else.

I took Ted's full name and address and thanked him for his honesty, saying I'd have to report the matter to my sergeant for advice. I informed him that I believed there were no grounds for prosecuting him for robbery, but did stress that I could not be sure.

The duty sergeant, who was not Sergeant Blaketon that day, could not decide the issue either, so he sought advice from the Inspector. I told the story as Ted had given it to me, and the Inspector said:

'Enter the wallet in the found property book, Rhea. We've had no complaint from anyone about being robbed, so that means there's no crime. If we record it as found property, it'll go into our records.'

'And if it's not claimed within three months, sir, it'll go back to Ted Donaldson?'

But we did not let it rest there. We told the local paper, who printed the pictures of the girl, and it transpired that a youth in Scarborough had been robbed of his wallet by two men a week earlier . . .

Ted had simply recovered the wallet from the thief.

But, I often mused, supposed Ted's victim had been

innocent and had complained that he had been robbed. Was there a criminal intent in Ted's mind at that moment?

4

A lost thing I could never find.

Hilaire Belloc, 1870–1953

The bewildering variety and massive quantity of objects which are recorded in the Found Property Register of any seaside police station is matched only by the variety and number which are recorded in the Lost Property Register. The snag is that the two registers seldom tally, for what is lost is seldom found, and what is found is seldom claimed.

This phenomenon is one of life's great mysteries, and it is one with which seaside police officers are especially familiar. By the end of every summer season, all corners of the police office are crammed with objects which no one has claimed or is likely to claim, and the range of property is truly amazing. How could anyone lose a wedding cake and never claim it? Or a pair of trousers or a brassière? Or their wallet, handbag, purse or shoes? One man even lost a bus and forty-two passengers, because he'd forgotten where he'd left it – we located it in a nearby car-park.

So far as normal lost and found objects are concerned, it might be wise to briefly explain some of the police procedures. These are followed meticulously because police officers have found themselves accused of stealing found goods when in fact the owner was more than careless when he or she lost it, or the finder less than truthful. To deal carelessly with found property can cost a police officer his or her career.

A good example of the risks can be shown when a wallet is reported found. Suppose a man lost a wallet which contained his personal papers and £100 or so in cash. Another person finds it, steals the cash and throws away the empty wallet. A third person then finds it and hands it to the police. If the policeman does not immediately, and in the presence of the finder, check the contents down to the last piece of dust, either he or the honest finder could be accused of stealing that missing cash. It is difficult to prove otherwise.

Due to the wide range of immense temptations which surround this curious aspect of police work, the handling of found property is very tightly controlled by printed orders, internal regulations and a mass of paperwork which involves meticulous records and the careful issue of receipts.

Police involvement in this social problem probably arose through well-meaning people bringing objects into the police station which they had found and which they believed to be the proceeds of crime. For this reason, every item of found property is checked against lists of stolen goods. In my time at Strensford, this was a manual task; now it is done by computer on a far wider scale.

Property which is reported lost is entered into a Lost Property register, which is compared with the Found Property Register, and it is very gratifying, through this system, to restore some precious thing to a loser.

One reason for people reporting so much lost property is, I am sure, because they believe their goods have been stolen, rather than lost. Sadly, there is often no proof that a crime has been committed when something has gone missing, and so the object is recorded as 'lost' rather than stolen. One simple example is when a woman goes shopping with a purse sitting on top of her basket – when she wants to pay her bill, she finds it has gone. Has it been stolen or has she merely lost it? Who can tell? Without clear evidence of a theft, the object will be recorded as 'lost'.

It goes without saying that there is a tremendous amount of administrative work involved with both found and lost property, and most police forces operate very similar systems.

When an object is reported found and the owner of that object is not traceable, or the object is not likely to produce a risk of any sort, like a bomb, a gun, a small boy, a kitten or a box of apples going rotten, the police will ask the finder to retain it for up to three months. A report of the finding will be made, and the finder will be told that if the thing is not claimed within three months, he can keep it.

'Finder retains' is a lovely entry in the Found Property Register because it provides the solution to a lot of problems. For one thing, admin. problems are reduced, and space in the found property cupboard is saved.

Some finders, however, are determined not to retain the objects they find, which means they must be stored in the police station for three months in case the owner turns up. If he does turn up to claim his treasure, the problem is solved; if he doesn't, the property must be disposed of. The finder will be offered it, and if he does not want it, it will be disposed of in a manner appropriate to the object in question.

This well-tried system was truly tested when Mr Roderick Holroyd, a businessman from Halifax in the then West Riding of Yorkshire, found a set of false teeth. It was a full set in very good condition, and at first he thought he had annoyed a crab.

Roderick, a large and jolly gentleman, had taken time off during a business trip to Strensford so that he could roll up his trousers and for a few minutes paddle at the edge of the North Sea, just below Strensford Pier, where the sea was shallow enough for him to keep his smart grey suit dry. So he had pottered into the water and had allowed it to soothe his size 10s. He had enjoyed the caresses of the slimy seaweed, the feel of the shifting sands under his soles and the coolness of water about his ankles. Then something had clamped itself around his toes.

I can well imagine his terror but when he lifted his foot from its shifting base, he found a set of false teeth lying there, awash with sea-water and sand.

Recognizing them as high-quality masticators, he retrieved them from their briny resting place, put them in his pocket and, during his return to normal business routine, managed to locate me on patrol.

51

'Ah, constable,' he beamed as he came to rest before me. 'I've some found property to report,' and he produced the clean set of dentures from his pocket. As he told me the circumstances of his discovery, I cringed. I guessed the reaction I'd get from the station! But knowing the rules which surrounded this delicate topic, I could hardly advise him to forget them or to throw them into the harbour, and so I had to produce my pocketbook and make a full report of the occurrence.

I took the teeth from him and examined them. I hoped they might bear some kind of dentist's or manufacturer's identifying mark, but I found nothing.

I'm sure their maker could have identified them, but the expense and time involved in scouring the nation for their birthplace could hardly be justified in this instance. It was not as if we were engaged in a murder enquiry or the identification of a dead body.

'You keep them,' I said when I had recorded all the necessary information. 'And if they are not claimed within three months, they are yours.'

He backed off rapidly, leaving me holding the teeth.

'Oh, no, constable. I don't want them. I just thought some poor devil would be wandering around Strensford unable to chew his whelks. They'll surely be reported lost at your office, won't they? And you can restore them to the loser . . . Goodbye . . .'

And thus I was lumbered with this unattractive item of found property. I shuddered to think of the reaction from the duty sergeant when I presented the teeth to him for official documentation and for issue of a receipt to Mr Holroyd. But it was not my task to question official procedures.

'Rhea!' Sergeant Blaketon was duty sergeant this afternoon. 'You blithering idiot. Who in their right mind would accept these from a finder? You realize what this means? It means records, receipts, these teeth occupying valuable space in the found property cupboard for three months, then letters to the finder to ask if he wants to have them back . . .'

'I was just following Standing Orders, sergeant,' I shrank beneath his onslaught, for I knew he could not argue against

52

this. Rules were his forte, he lived by rules and regulations, and so there was no way out of this dilemma.

He had to accept the teeth and he had to initiate the necessary procedures. I left him to it.

No one came to report losing them or to claim ownership, and during my three months at Strensford they remained on the front of a shelf in the cupboard, grinning at all who placed further items there. Shortly before I completed my tour, the three necessary 'finders' months were complete, and no one had claimed the teeth.

'Rhea,' said Sergeant Blaketon one morning. 'I've got a job for you.'

'Yes, sergeant,' I stood before him in the office.

'You can send an official form to your Mr Holroyd to inform him that three months have expired since he reported finding those false teeth and that, as no one has claimed them, they now officially belong to him. Ask him to come and collect them. Then we can get the things written off.'

And so I completed the necessary forms and posted them to the finder. Mr Holroyd rang the office next day just after 10 a.m., and by chance Sergeant Blaketon and I were there, working an early shift.

Blaketon took the call and listened carefully. I heard him trying to persuade Mr Holroyd to collect the teeth next time he was in town, but he declined. He wanted nothing more to do with them. And then I heard Oscar Blaketon ask, 'In that case, have we your authority to dispose of them?'

The answer was clearly in the affirmative because Sergeant Blaketon endorsed the register 'Finder declines to accept after three-month period, and authorizes police to dispose of this item of property.'

'There, Rhea,' he said. 'This little seaside saga is almost over. Now, here's your teeth!'

'They're not mine, sergeant!'

'You will dispose of them,' he said to me ominously. 'That's an order. We have the official owner's permission. It's all in the books. So there you are, take them and get rid of them.'

And he pressed them into the palm of my hand, now wrapped neatly in some tissue paper.

'Yes, sergeant,' I had to agree. I stuffed them into my uniform pocket and made a mental note to dispose of them in the station dustbin. But by the time he had finished instructing me about car-parking problems, bus-parking problems, youngsters in pubs and the illicit dropping of litter, I had forgotten about the teeth. I walked to my beat and passed the station dustbin *en route*.

A few minutes later, I found myself patrolling along the harbourside. It was when I arrived at the very place where I had been handed those teeth three months ago that I remembered them and became very aware of them sitting in my pocket. I removed the tissue package and simultaneously smelt the briny harbour water. A brisk breeze wafted the scents of the sea towards me, and I recalled that the teeth had been rescued from a watery grave. Quite impulsively, I felt that a return to the ocean would be eminently suitable for these teeth. It was far better than a dustbin, I felt, far more permanent and almost symbolic.

I moved into the shelter of a herring shed and then, making sure I was not observed, flung the teeth far across the harbour. With immense satisfaction, I saw them plop into the water and sink out of sight. The file was closed.

I resumed my patrol, glad it was all over.

Five minutes later, a small gentleman hailed me.

'Oh, er, excuse me, officer,' he began. 'Can I mention something to you?'

'Yes, of course.'

'Well, it's a bit funny, I suppose, but, well, three months ago I was on holiday here, a short break you know. And well, I went for a swim, just below the pier. I'm not much of a swimmer really and swallowed a lot of water, a huge gulp it was. Well, I coughed and spluttered and lost my false teeth in the sea, you understand. They just shot out, a new set.

'I looked all over but didn't find them, and, well, friends said I should have reported it to the police, just in case they'd been found. But you see I live a long way off and had to rush for my bus, and then, well, this is the first time I've been back to Strensford, so when I saw you, I thought I'd mention it. I don't suppose they have been found, have they? I mean, it would be odd, wouldn't it? A chance in thousands, really, but, well, I thought it might be worth asking . . . You never know, do you?'

'No, you never can tell,' I agreed, taking out my pocketbook to make a note of the matter.

Much found property is of little cash value, and it has more of a sentimental meaning to its loser. But there are times when the situation changes. I am reminded of an incident which occurred as I was patrolling the harbourside one fine August afternoon on my first spell of duty in Strensford, some years before this visit.

I spotted a roadsweeper moving steadily towards me. He was a small, chubby fellow with a flat cap and a dark-blue shirt with the sleeves rolled up. He was manœuvring a barrow which was really a dustbin on wheels. This was the tool of his trade, and it contained a space for his brush and shovel. With the stiff-bristled brush, he was sweeping litter from the gutters and footpaths. It was a thankless task but he was obviously anxious to make Strensford as smart and as clean as possible, in spite of visitors' efforts to frustrate him.

I don't think he was aware of my presence barely a few yards ahead of him as he slowly moved about his careful work. With his head down, he kept his eyes on the road and the gutters, and his mind upon his solitary task. He swept all before him until it formed a medium-sized pile, and then, after removing his shovel from its resting-place on his barrow, he collected the debris and dropped it into his bin. His work was slow and methodical.

As I carelessly observed him, not really watching him but being merely aware of his presence, he scooped up a shovelful of waste and placed it inside his bin. Then he halted his routine and delved deep inside the bin; this change of action and routine caused me to take a little more interest. I saw him lift out a bundle of paper. From a distance, it looked like a screwed-up mass of newspaper or other white paper with printing upon it, but he was making a very careful study of it. Then he glanced around, noticed me and began to walk quickly in my direction, holding the bundle as if it was hot.

'Look,' he said. 'It's money. Fivers. Ah've just fun 'em in t'gutter.'

I took the bundle from him, and sure enough, they were £5 notes of the large, white variety, now obsolete but then very much in vogue. One of them represented something approaching a week's wages for some workers. With the little fellow watching, I expressed my amazement and then carefully counted them before his eyes.

There was a total of sixty notes, £300 in all, very close to a year's wages for the roadman, and not far off a year's wages for me either!

'Phew!' I breathed. 'You found all this money, down there in the gutter?'

'Aye,' he grinned weak smile, a nervous one almost and showed thick, brown teeth. 'Just there, sweeping up. Noticed 'em on my shovel, just in time.'

'We'll have to report the find,' I informed him. 'Can you come with me now, to the station? I think you ought to be present when I record this.'

'Ah've all this length to finish before knocking-off time,' he said.

'I think that can wait, under the circumstances.'

I wanted him to come to the station for two reasons. First, in view of the amount involved, I felt he ought to be there when the official procedures were set in motion, and secondly, it was more than likely that someone had already reported the loss of such an amount. If so, the money could be very quickly restored to its rightful owner, and there might be a reward for the sweeper. He agreed to come along with me, albeit with some reluctance, and so we proceeded through the streets, with the little fellow in firm control of his barrow and with me hiding the wadge of notes in my uniform pocket.

At the station, a Sergeant Moreton was on duty and looked in amazement as I entered with the roadman.

'An arrest is it?' he asked as I entered the office.

'No, sergeant, it's found property,' I said.

I told my story, after which I plonked the £300 on the counter before him. His eyebrows rose in surprise and he looked at the roadman with admiration.

'Enter it in the register, son. Now, in view of the amount involved, we cannot let the finder retain this. But, strange though it may seem, we've had no report of a loss. Not yet. I suppose there's time for that. And, if there is no report of a loss, it will go to the finder, and that'll make you a rich man, eh?'

The roadman smiled briefly. I went through the formalities, recording that his name was Lawrence Briggs who was employed by the council as a roadsweeper and who was sixty-four years old. He had an address on the council estate across the river. I explained the formalities to him and told him that if the money was not claimed within three months, it would be his.

'It'll be a nice retirement present,' he said quietly.

'You're retiring soon, are you?' I asked.

'November,' he said. 'When I'm sixty-five.'

'If this isn't claimed, it could give you a holiday,' I suggested.

'New furniture more like,' he said. 'Me and the missus has never had much, not on my wage. I'd love a television and some good furniture, a nice settee . . .'

'It was very honest of you to report that money,' I commented. 'I'd bet some wouldn't have.'

'Aye, well, mebbe so. But I'm honest, officer. Somebody'll have lost that and it'll mean more to them than me. No, I wouldn't dream of keeping it.'

'OK, well, it's in safe hands now. So if it's not claimed within three months, we'll be in touch with you and you can come and collect it.'

He smiled and left the office, and I saw him trundling his barrow down the cobbled hill and back into the busy streets. With luck, he'd get his length finished by knocking-off time, but I did find myself marvelling at his honesty.

'You know, son,' said Sergeant Moreton two hours later. 'This is very odd. No one's reported losing that cash, not a whisper. It's a fortune, you know; I mean, what sort of person carries that amount with him, let alone loses it and doesn't say anything?'

Like Sergeant Moreton, I could only marvel at the story but knew we dare not publicize the finding, otherwise all kinds of dishonest folks would suddenly 'remember' losing the money.

But in time someone did report its loss. The call came later that evening.

'It's Bridlington Police,' announced the caller. 'Sergeant Youngman speaking. Now, have you had a report of any cash being found in Strensford? A lot of cash. In notes. Fivers. I don't expect you to say you have, because if anyone found it, they'd say nowt.'

'Yes, sergeant,' I said. 'We have had some found.'

'£300 in fivers, was it?'

'Yes, it was found close to the harbourside.'

'Then I've got a very relieved loser here right now. He lost £300 in fivers today. He's a Mr George Kenton from Surrey. He came to Strensford on the SS *Princess* from Bridlington today and, when he got back on the boat for the return trip, realized he had lost his holiday cash. He couldn't report it until the boat returned to harbour here, and well, he came straight to our office to tell us. I'll ask him to come over to Strensford as soon as possible to collect the money. Now, who's the honest character who found it?'

I explained how the roadsweeper had found the cash and provided his name and address. Sergeant Youngman said he would inform the loser of those details. Mr Kenton would come tonight, I was told, so after thanking Sergeant Youngman for his call, I made a note in the Occurrence Book so that the next shift would be aware of the situation.

I went off duty before the money was handed over to its rightful owner, and it seems he arrived late that evening to claim his cash. It was handed over against his signature and the matter was closed.

But he did not leave even a shilling reward for the road-sweeper. There was not a penny and not even a letter of thanks for his honesty. We all knew that he would not wish any thanks or a reward but would gain satisfaction from knowing that his honesty had been ratified by the money going to its rightful owner.

We waited a few days, but nothing came, and so Sergeant Moreton, who was friendly with the local reporter on the *Strensford Gazette*, decided to tell the tale to the papers. If Kenton was not going to give some reward, the story of the roadman's honest was strong enough for the local and even the national papers. And so it won headlines in some papers and more than a few column inches in others, and we made sure a copy was sent to Kenton at his home address. But not even that prompted a response.

Happily, although the publicity did not prompt a response from Kenton, there was a small but touching flood of postal orders, cash and cheques for the roadman from readers all over England. If the loser did not appreciate his remarkable honesty, the public did. All the police officers at Strensford had a whip-round for him too, and he was able to buy himself a new settee with those generous donations.

Another odd use of the Found Property Register occurred late one night when I was working a night shift during that three-month spell of duty. I was sitting in the office around 2.15 a.m. having my break when a rather rough-looking, brusquely spoken character presented himself at the enquiry desk.

His name was Brian Stockfield, a taxi-driver in his early forties who was renowned in the town for his bad temper, his loud voice and awful, critical treatment of his fellow men. No one had a good word for Stockfield; he complained incessantly about everything, criticizing the council because of the rates, the police for letting holiday-makers park all over the town, the holiday-makers for crowding the streets, the children for their noise, dogs for barking . . . Every facet of Strensford's society was criticized by this chap, and the outcome was that those who knew him kept out of his way. He had not been in Strensford during my initial spell, so I had never come across him until now.

Stockfield earned his living by running a one-vehicle taxi business, and his premises were a small wooden garage close to the harbourside. He criticized other taxi-drivers for taking business from him, he wrote to the newspaper about their activities and claimed that some had not taken out the correct insurance for their vehicles, or that their hackney carriage licences were not in order. He was a regular caller at the police station, where his growing list of complaints was logged. In short, he was nothing but a confounded nuisance to everyone.

It was through chats with the local police that I discovered one of his unpleasant traits – perhaps, though, he had just cause for this particular behaviour.

When the police in Strensford came across a drunk who was not troublesome or a danger either to himself or to anyone else, they hailed a local taxi and persuaded the driver to take the drunk home. This system was very sensible, because it kept the cells empty, it saved the drunk from the trauma of a prosecution, it saved the police a lot of work and the courts a lot of time dealing with simple drunks. Furthermore, it helped to retain the friendly relationship between the residents and the police, for the people would resent any heavy-handed treatment of local merrymakers. It made a lot of sense to deal with them in this gentle way. Another aspect was that it kept all the taxi-drivers in business too, because they made useful, honest sums from their merry fares.

The system had a lot to commend it, but Brian Stockfield would not partake in it. He complained about the drunks, about their noise, their singing and their general conduct. He would not have anything at all to do with them. But this did not unduly worry the other taxi-drivers, who were happy to accommodate our discarded drunks. His financial loss was their gain.

On this night, as he arrived at the police station counter, I learned, he had answered such a call, and that was the reason for his presence. He had another complaint to make.

PC Joe Tapley, a local constable of considerable experience, was the office duty man that night, and he went to the counter to deal with Stockfield. I and three colleages sat near the fireside, enjoying our meal, and we were just beyond the vision of the visitor. But we could hear every word.

'Ah, Mr Stockfield,' greeted PC Tapley. 'What brings you to us at this late hour?'

'I have a complaint to make,' he said. 'About a clever sod who's been to a dance at the Imperial Hotel.'

'Not paid his fare?' suggested Joe Tapley.

'Paid? Yes, he's paid. It's bloody awful, Mr Tapley, terrible really, what folks do to your taxis.'

'Oh, like that, is it? So what's he done?'

Joe had a pad of notepaper handy and was preparing to record the problem.

'Look, Mr Tapley, you know what I'm like with drunks, don't you? You and the lads. I go for class clients, not drunks. My vehicle is the cleanest taxi in town, even though I say so myself. None of my fares can complain about me running a mucky vehicle.'

'Go on, Mr Stockfield.' I noticed the formal exchange of names between these two, indicative of some past conflict.

'I got this call, right? From a chap attending the Imperial Hunt Ball, it is. He had a nice accent, and it is a class dance, as you know. Even though he sounded a bit fuzzy, a bit slurred when he spoke, I went for him. I picked him up at 1.30 a.m., on the dot, and took him to the Grand Hotel, where he's staying.'

'And he paid?'

'Yes, he paid. Charming he was, all done up in an evening-dress suit, a right toff.'

'Your ideal client, eh?'

'You would think so, wouldn't you?'

'So what is your complaint, Mr Stockfield?' asked PC Tapley.

'Well, I find this very embarrassing. I'm a clean-living, clean-speaking man, Mr Tapley, but, well, he's used the back seat of my taxi as a toilet.'

'You mean he's peed on it?' I could discern the merest flicker of a smile on Joe Tapley's face, and he was doing his best to suppress it.

'No, the other. Two massive great brown turds, like a dog's, on the back seat. You come and see for yourself, and don't stick your nose in either. The smell is bloody awful.'

Joe followed him outside, and so we all trooped out as well, for this would be a sight to treasure. Sure enough, as Stockfield switched on the interior light, the centre of the back seat was graced by two shining examples of man's slavery to the urgent needs of nature. They were a pair of thick, brown turds.

We were all creasing ourselves with laughter, and happily the darkness of the night concealed most of our efforts to keep straight faces, but Joe achieved it with aplomb. He led us all back inside, and we seated ourselves at the fireside again, leaving Joe to finalize the matter.

'Well,' demanded Stockfield. 'What are you going to do about it?'

'Do you know the man's name? The chap who left it?'

'No, he's a visitor. I doubt if I would recognize him again. He was just a bloke who wanted a lift home from a dance.'

'Hmm,' said Joe writing on the scrap pad. 'Name and description unknown.' When he had finished writing, he said, 'Well, thank you, Mr Stockfield. I have made a note of all the relevant details. Thank you for calling.'

'But what are you going to do about it?' demanded the taxi-driver, whose voice was beginning to grow louder.

'Do?' smiled Joe calmly. 'Nothing else. I've done all that I can. I have made a record of the event in our Found Property Register. If the owner cannot be traced, and if the property is not claimed within three months, you may keep it. As things are, you may now take it home and await any likely claim of ownership. We will keep the matter of file for three months too.'

'Found property?' cried Stockfield. 'You can't call this found property?'

'Then what else is it?' smiled Joe, as calm as ever. 'No crime has been committed, no byelaw broken, no traffic regulation breached, no street nuisance committed, no indecent public exhibition. It's simply a case of someone unknown leaving something rather personal in your taxi. And thank you for reporting it. Goodnight, Mr Stockfield.'

He left without a word, and we waited until the sound of his revving engine faded before collapsing into bouts of laughter. There is a lot to be learned from an experienced police officer.

5

Animals are such agreeable friends,
They ask no questions, they pass no criticism.

George Eliot, 1819–80

Night duty can be very lonely. After the pubs have closed, the restaurants have cleared their tables and the clubs have bolted their doors, the streets rapidly empty and there is little companionship for the patrolling constable. His solitary work, which in my case began at 10 p.m. and finished at 6 a.m., comprised the checking of lock-up premises and empty houses and a general watching brief on the sleeping town. I kept my ears open for those who prowled at night, for burglars and shop-breakers, for vagrants and other ne'er-do-wells whose illegal activities were conducted under the cover of darkness.

More often than not, nothing of this kind ever happened. There were few burglars and nocturnal villains to arrest or deter, and the resultant boredom was often relieved only by the appearance of the night duty sergeant or sometimes an inspector, with, very occasionally, the eminence of the super-intendent himself. In the momentary absence of those super-visory officers, the constables would gather at some suitable place for a chat, flashing coded messages to one another by torch and making use of reflections from shop windows to pass our morse-like messages along streets and around corners.

There were times, however, when the exigencies of the service and the wanderings of supervisory officers meant that such meetings could not be arranged. This inevitably meant that the long hours after midnight became very, very lonely and excruciatingly boring, so that a companion of some kind, any kind, was most welcome.

At 1 a.m. on such a morning, I stood forlornly outside the GPO in the town centre of Strensford. I was making a point at the telephone kiosk and was feeling very melancholy as I longed for my meal break which was scheduled for 2.15 a.m. Then I'd be able to have a few minutes chat and banter with my colleagues, all of which would be washed down with hot coffee from my flask and fortified with some of my landlady's sandwiches.

As I waited in the chill of that summer night, I became aware of a dog trotting along the street towards me. He was a stocky animal, a mature yellow labrador, and he was completely alone. I said nothing as I watched, and then he noticed me in the dim glow of the kiosk and headed in my direction. Without any hint of indecision, he came and sat at my side, his tail thumping the pavement in greeting.

'Hello, boy,' I acknowledged him. 'Who are you then?'

I fingered his collar, but it bore no name or address of his owner, nor his own name. But he was a solid-looking, well-fed dog in excellent condition and, I guessed, about five or six years old. He made a small fuss when I patted him but sat at my side almost as if he had been trained to do so. I spoke to him and used words like 'go home', but he did not shift his position until it was time for me to leave.

I now had twenty-five minutes of further patrolling before my next point at the New Quay telephone kiosk, and this would be occupied by checking the shops, back and front, and inspecting all the dark corners of the myriad of quaint passages which were such a feature of Strensford's ancient town centre. They were called yards, and the police nightly examined them for sleeping tramps, drunks, people who might be ill or lost, or villains who might be lurking there hoping to break into a shop or hotel through the back windows or doors.

When my five minutes' wait at the GPO was over, I said, 'Well, boy, I must go. I've a lot to do. Goodbye.'

But as I walked away, he followed. He walked at my heels on

the right-hand side, his tail gently wagging with the swaying movement of his thick-set body. He was just like a trained police dog, and yet I had no idea where he had come from.

I decided to see just how carefully trained he really was. To carry out my little test, I stopped at the entrance to one of these dark and almost sinister yards and listened. He stopped at my side and sat down, ears alert. I had not given him any command.

Now I had to enter that dark and narrow tunnel-like passage to check dozens of shop premises, pubs and warehouses whose rear doors or windows were accessible from there, and consequently very accessible for an attack. It was a nightly task; armed only with a torch I had to check every pane of glass, and every cranny for lurking crooks. Without a personal radio set, I was alone and vulnerable. If I was attacked by burglars or layabouts, there was no way I could call my colleagues for help, other than by blowing my whistle, if I had time, or just shouting loudly in the hope that someone somewhere would respond. But now it seemed that I had some welcome assistance.

'Seek, boy,' I said to the dog, and off he went. Tail wagging and ears alert, he went ahead of me into the long, dark passage, and I waited at the entrance. The seconds ticked away and there was no sound, not even a reassuring bark or a cat scuttling for safety, so I allowed a full two minutes. Still with no sound or sign of him, I shone my torch into the dark void and, seeing nothing, decided that my companion of but a few moments ago had left me and that he'd gone home. Once more I was alone, so I entered the passage aided by the light of my torch, and there he was, trotting towards me in fine spirits. He wagged his tail in welcome, turned around and led me through the dank darkness.

As I checked all the premises along my route, he remained with me. He spent his time sniffing at doors, dustbins and windows and entering dark corners, outhouses, external toilets and similar dark structures well ahead of me. If there had been anyone hiding in those secret places, the labrador would have flushed them out or certainly located them.

For the next hour, he remained with me, always walking at heel without being commanded when I was patrolling the streets and open spaces but going ahead to search the alleys, yards and dark recesses of the town whenever I said, 'Seek boy.'

He was a remarkable dog, and I wondered what he would do when I went into the police station for my break. As the long-awaited hour of 2.15 a.m. approached, I made my way across Station Square to the welcoming lights of the old police station, and the dog followed, always at heel and never straying. But when I approached the side-street door which always stood half-open at night, he rushed ahead of me, pushed open the door and hurried inside. I followed down the steps into the depths of this Victorian pile and was in time to see him curling up beneath the counter, settling down for a snooze close to the fireside of the cosy office.

When I joined my colleagues for my break, Joe Tapley asked, 'Has Rusty been with you tonight, Nick?'

'Rusty?' for the briefest of moments, I thought he was referring to one of the local officers.

'The dog, that labrador. We call him Rusty.'

'Oh,' I smiled. 'Yes, he picked me up at one o'clock and has been with me ever since. Is he yours?'

'No,' he laughed. 'No, although sometimes I wish he was. He's a wonderful chap, aren't you, Rusty?'

The dog lifted his head and acknowledged the compliment by flapping his tail several times on the floor.

'Where does he come from?' I asked, opening my sandwiches and flask.

'Dunno,' said Joe, shrugging his shoulders. 'None of us knows. He just turns up from time to time, selects one of us for his patrol and then walks the beat until six o'clock. Then he goes home. The trouble is, we don't know who he belongs to or where he goes. We call him Rusty, and he responds. He'll search all your awkward spots for you, you know. Just say "Seek Rusty" and off he'll go. He could be the official Strensford Police Dog.'

'Don't his owners ever miss him?'

'No, I don't suppose they know he comes out at night. I imagine they shut him in some outbuilding for the night, and by the time they open up next morning he'll be back in residence.

It's almost as if he had this secret life helping us, being a Special Constable really. He's great, a marvellous companion on nights.'

'Doesn't he show up in the daytime then?' I asked.

'No, never. He'll come to town several nights during a month, not every night, mind. He'll select one of the lads to be his companion during his night patrol and will stick with him all night. Then he'll wander off home. He's obviously from a good home because he's so well fed, and he won't eat with us either. He wouldn't touch our sandwiches, although sometimes he'll take a drink of water.'

'Has anyone tried to follow him home?'

'Not really. By six o'clock we're all shattered and ready for bed, besides we're all on foot anyway. He trots off and there's no way we could keep pace with him. He lives out of town, we know that, so we think he's from one of the nearby villages or farms. But beyond that we don't know where he hails from.'

At 3 a.m. I was due to commence the second half of my shift, and as I moved from my chair to pack away my things and rinse out my flask, Rusty opened his eyes, thumped his tail and joined me. I gave him a saucer of water, which he lapped happily, and then we resumed our joint patrol.

He remained with me until a few minutes before 6 a.m.; as before, he checked all the yards and passages ahead of me and helped me enormously during that shift. Then, as I made my final slow, tired walk across the town to book off duty, he suddenly veered away from me and began to trot away.

'Goodnight, Rusty,' I called after him, and he turned his head, wagged his tail and departed. Two minutes later, he was out of sight.

During my short spell of duty in Strensford, I was accompanied by Rusty on four of five occasions. He came more often, of course, and seemed to share himself between the other patrolling constables.

Of the happy memories which I shall always associate with him, two stand out. On one occasion, about 1.30 a.m., I despatched him down an alley to carry out his customary search, and this time he barked. It was a warning bark, and it was followed by a shout of alarm following which a youth bustled out of the darkness, dragging a girl with him.

He was one of the local small-time crooks, whom I recognized, and although I checked all the nearby premises and found them secure, I guessed Rusty had prevented a 'breaking' job that night. No doubt the girl was being used as a form of cover by the youth, and her (probably innocent) presence with him was designed to make the police believe he was merely courting. But I recorded the fact and his name in my notebook and left a detailed account for the CID, should any subsequent premises be entered.

Soon after that little episode, I was on day-time patrol and was asked by another local crook whether police dogs were operating in Strensford. Word of Rusty's presence had obviously got around, so I said,

'Yes, but they're not Alsatians. They don't look like ordinary police dogs; they're CID – canines in disguise.'

I don't know what he made of that information but I guessed it would circulate among the small-time crooked fraternity of Strensford.

The other memorable incident with Rusty occurred during the early hours of a chill morning, around 3 a.m. It was, in fact, the last time we patrolled together, and he had selected me for his companion during that night shift. I was finding the long, second half very tiring and was almost asleep on my feet as, with his help, I was checking shops and yards in another part of town.

I arrived at the entrance to Sharpe's Yard, which led off Shunnergate, and sent Rusty about his usual mission. He came back without barking, which I interpreted as the all-clear signal. I knew that no villains lurked down there. Nonetheless, I had to make my own search in case there were broken windows or signs of illicit entry to the rear of the shops.

With my torch lighting the windows above me, I began my journey, but after only a dozen strides, Rusty was before me, growling and barking. His noise filled the air and jerked me into wakefulness. I stopped immediately.

Was someone waiting down here? Something had alarmed

him.

The hairs on the nape of my neck stood erect as the light of my torch searched the corners and ledges before me and above me. I could see nothing to cause me concern.

'It's all right, Rusty,' I said. 'There's nothing.'

I started to walk again, but once more he barked. I stopped and this time shone my torch upon him.

He was standing near the front edge of a gaping hole, his voice warning me not to walk into it. Someone had lifted an inspection cover to a draining system and had left it propped against the wall. A hole some seven or eight feet deep, with iron steps leading down, lay before me.

'Rusty!' I crouched on my haunches and hugged him, and he seemed to understand my gratitude. I replaced the cover and, feeling rather shaken at what might have occurred, concluded my night's patrol.

As always, just before six o'clock, Rusty trotted away. I shouted, 'Thanks, Rusty,' as he moved rapidly out of my sight, but he never looked back, and that was the last time we patrolled together.

I never saw him again. I did puzzle over the kind of formal training he had undergone because it had clearly been very thorough, and the incident with the missing inspection cover did make me wonder if he'd ever been trained as a guide dog for a blind person.

Even to this day, I do not know where he came from or who owned him, and perhaps I never will. But he was a lovely companion, a sincere friend, a super dog and a very good police officer.

I shall never forget him.

During that short sojourn to the coast, I had several memorable experiences with animals, most of which occurred during my night patrols.

It was a regular occurrence, for example, for animals to escape from their compounds at the slaughterhouse. It was almost as if they were aware of their impending fate and were making a last, desperate effort to escape and, hopefully, survive.

It frequently happened that night-duty policemen were the first to know of these escapes, and it became their responsibility to arrange for the capture of the fleeing animals. In my short time there, a pig got loose, a sheep escaped, a young bullock absconded and a cow managed to free itself.

The pig and the sheep caused no real problems because they were easily rounded up, although their moments of blissful freedom did entail wild and noisy gallops through the streets with posse-like constables in hot pursuit on foot or cycle. I do know that one such chase, with a very noisy pig as the target, aroused several streets of slumbering residents and many bewildered holiday-makers, some of whom thought that Count Dracula had come to the town. A screeching pig can produce a most unholy noise.

In spite of the noise, the general idea was simply to corner the animal, secure it and return it protesting to its death chamber.

The cow was rather different. She was bigger for a start, and when a cow takes fright and blunders about the streets at night, she can demolish shop windows, damage cars, leap into sitting-rooms and do all manner of wild and irresponsible acts which amount to genuine vandalism. So a rampaging cow has to be quickly halted, and sadly the solution is often a powerful rifle.

This particular cow, a hornless Red Poll of a delightful chestnut colour, was such an animal. In the thrill of the chase, she turned into a galloping powerhouse of beef, and we sensed tragedy if she wasn't halted in her tracks.

To cut a long story short, we knocked out of bed a member of the local Rifle Club, a territorial army firearms instructor, who joined the hunt with a .303 rifle. We drove the terrified beast into the coal yard, where she was put out of her misery by one well-aimed shot to the head.

The bullock was a similar problem, but he, being a lively young lad, took a good deal more catching than the cow of previous weeks. He was smaller for one thing, faster for another and very cunning too.

He was spotted in a shopping arcade by one of the patrolling constables, and seemed docile enough. He was not galloping aimlessly about the place, so the constable rang the office and alerted the sergeant, who in turn recruited the rest of us as reluctant matadors. We all set off in pursuit of the bullock, a handsome Hereford. His large, flat white face was like a beacon in the darkness, and it caught the light from the few street lamps as he moved casually about the town with us in close attendance. This had not yet developed into a chase, it was more like easy cattle-droving, for we were endeavouring to persuade him to walk into some enclosed space.

The snag is that town centres are not rich with enclosed spaces of the kind that will accommodate a frisky young bullock, and as he moved about the streets, we racked our brains as we sought a suitable paddock. Then the sergeant recalled Cragdale Hall, a large, deserted mansion close to the town centre. It had large iron gates and a high surrounding wall which provided a total enclosure, and the house was empty too. It was surrounded by overgrown lawns and gardens and was an ideal place to contain a bullock. He sent one of the constables ahead to open the gates in preparation, and the rest of us were briefed to guide the bullock in that general direction.

Things went very well until the bullock turned into one of the dark yards which riddle the town centre. These are long and narrow and link one street with another which runs parallel to it. As the bullock turned into the narrow entrance, the sergeant yelled.

'Two of you, get to the other end. Hold him in. We've got him.'

Two young constables ran ahead and disappeared down one of the adjoining yards, and we could hear them galloping along its echoing sandstone base. Then we heard the galloping of hooves followed by a shout of alarm, and it seems that as those two policemen emerged at the distant end of their yard, a shop-breaker, complete with his illicit haul, with a young bull hard on his heels, emerged with some speed and anxiety from the adjoining yard.

He had just climbed out of a rear ground-floor window of the Co-Op as the bullock arrived at that point; I did wonder if he thought the police had recruited bulls as well as dogs for such duties, although I imagine he never gave it a thought, at least not just then. However, his shout of alarm had frightened our quarry; it caused the bullock to begin a fast gallop hard behind the worried shop-breaker, who immediately ran for his life. The pair of them sped from the end of that yard like two peas exploding from a peashooter, the crook maintaining the slenderest of leads.

And the shop-breaker had the wit not to release his haul, which comprised a large carton of cigarettes, the result being that he was caught red-handed. Happily, the constables who emerged from the adjoining yard at about the same moment were quick enough to appreciate the situation and grabbed the villain, while the bullock did its best to avoid the drama and vanished towards the harbourside.

As the two happy arresters escorted their man to the police station, the remaining matadors pursued their quarry at a sedate pace, not wishing to panic him into a burst of sudden activity. Their droving skills directed him along the edge of the harbour, and we were delighted when he entered one of the herring sheds. We reckoned we could contain him there while the owner of the slaughterhouse was contacted; and so we did. The man arrived shortly afterwards with a cattle-truck and two of his own men. With remarkable ease, they persuaded the bullock to enter it.

And that was that. The excitement was over, except that I wonder how many shop-breakers have been arrested by a bullock on night duty.

Another interesting hunt was started by a drunk who rang the police station about half-past eleven one warm summer night to say that he had seen a ferocious unidentified beast on the harbour wall and that it had washed its supper in the harbour water before vanishing below deck on one of the fishing cobles.

Unlikely as it seemed, it was a good enough yarn to be relayed to the policeman who was patrolling the harbourside, and he promised to keep his eyes open. Half an hour later, he rang the office to confirm the sighting. There *was* a peculiar animal upon the boats, and he had no idea what it was. He said it was about as

big as a badger and of a nondescript colour so far as he could see;
but it wasn't a badger, and it was jumping from one boat to the
next. It certainly looked dangerous.

All the night-duty constables, including myself, were told to
volunteer to help catch the fearsome thing before it spread
rabies or did some other irreparable harm to the town. To help
in this task, we recruited the fire brigade, the fishermen themselves and anyone else who could be found at that time of night.
This resulted in all the drunks from the harbourside pubs
volunteering, along with many strolling holiday-makers and
several motorists who shone their car lights across the resting
boats which bobbed and swayed on the water.

Some of the fishermen had the bright idea of driving it
towards a wall of fishing nets which they would hold up, and so
the trap was set. At this point, we weren't really sure where it
was, and we certainly didn't know what it was, which meant we
didn't know what it might do. Nonetheless, we all boarded the
boats and began to beat upon their wooden decks, hoping to
flush out the beast.

Under lights beaming down from the boats' masts and in the
glow of car headlamps, we set about our mission, and it is fair to
say that there was a good deal of nervousness which was hidden
among the noise and laughter. None of us knew whether he was
going to be savaged by some ghastly creature from another
country as the noisy, bawdy hunt continued.

Suddenly, the large furry thing bolted from below deck and
scurried across one of the boats. Accompanied by shouting and
banging on buckets and dustbin lids, it sped from deck to deck,
crossing the fleet of fishing cobles with remarkable dexterity
and avoiding the outstretched fishing nets until it was able to
leap onto the side of the harbour wall. Then, remarkably, it
clung to the seaweed and stones of the wall and somehow
scuttled along the side of the wall until we saw it disappear
beneath the wooden flooring of the pier extension.

'What is it?' asked someone when that minor panic was over.

'Dunno, but it looks like a giant bloody rat!' said one man.
'I've not seen owt like yon, never. And it has a bushy tail. Rats
haven't bushy tails, leastways not ships' rats.'

The police officers present gathered to discuss the next phase of the operation, and Sergeant White, on duty that night, asked:

'Right, you all saw it. What was it?'

Our answers ranged from a giant mouse to a giant cat, by way of a monster mongoose or a massive squirrel. It was about the size of a badger, that was not in dispute, but the darkness of the night and the animal's rapid movements made it impossible to get a clear view of it. We all agreed that it seemed to be a brownish grey colour, although the darkness made it difficult to make a proper assessment. Someone said its tail was bushy, and black and white, and we all felt it wasn't either a dog or a fox, nor even a badger. Such animals could never cling to the side of the harbour wall in the remarkable manner it had shown.

Now, however, it was somewhere under the pier extension, probably clambering over the mass of steel supports and girders. At least it was isolated to a degree, and if it emerged from there, we would be able to see it.

Sergeant White spoke. 'PC Rhea, go to a telephone kiosk and ring Gerard Bright,' he announced. 'He's got the pet shop. His home number will be in the directory. Tell him what's happened – he might know what it is and what to do. Then report back to me. I'll remain here and supervise.'

I rang Mr Bright from the fishmarket kiosk, and he asked me to explain all that I knew. I relayed a tale of the chase and a varied descriptions of the animal which was based on all the garbled accounts I'd heard.

'Bloody hell!' I heard him exclaim. 'Hang on a minute, officer.'

He left the telephone and returned saying, 'I'll be down there right away. Don't chase it any more – leave it to me.'

I relayed this advice to Sergeant White, who called for all the hunters to keep back, to remain at a distance and under no circumstances to approach the animal. An expert was on the way, he announced with all the seriousness he could muster.

I tried to tell him that Mr Bright had not indicated the thing was dangerous, his advice being simply to leave it alone, but White was not taking any risks. He moved everyone back from the pier extension and waited. Somehow he managed to generate all the tension of a man-eating tiger hunt.

Mr Bright arrived on a pedal cycle and from the saddlebag lifted a vacuum flask of water, a dog's dish and two hard-boiled eggs.

'Right,' he said. 'Everyone keep back. I'm going for it.'

He walked to the end of the wooden pier extension, filled the bowl with water, put it on the ground and placed the eggs close to it. Then he shouted:

'Rocky, Rocky, Rocky.'

We all watched, breathless, and heard a scratching noise from beneath and then the head of a sharp-eared animal appeared. Then the rest of its body scrambled onto the surface of the extension and scuttled across to the eggs. It seized one, washed it in the water and settled down to eat it.

Mr Bright picked the creature up, and it snuggled against him as he carried it towards us.

'It's my pet racoon,' he said. 'He's escaped somehow. He's completely harmless, but very nervous when there is a lot of noise and shouting. Thank you for finding him.'

'It's a pleasure,' said Sergeant White. 'A real pleasure. Now, can we get the town back to normal?'

Of all the animals that have befriended mankind, the seaside donkey is surely one of the most lovable. Stubborn at times, their overall patience with tiny children is renowned, and a donkey ride remains one of the highlights of a day on the beach. Grouped together in small numbers, seaside donkeys spend their working lives plodding a well-worn path along the sands to the gleeful shouts of youngsters and the tinkling of bells on their harnesses. And then, in the winter, they are split into singles or perhaps pairs and despatched to inland farms, there to enjoy a few months relaxation. Lots of moorland farms are hosts to a donkey or two during the winter, and I recall a friend of mine riding two miles or so to primary school on a donkey which was boarded out at his father's farm.

The Strensford donkeys were no exception. There would be about fifteen of them, small patient beasts whose working day was like that of seaside donkeys everywhere.

They lived high on the cliff near the abbey, and each morning during the summer they were driven down the donkey path which dropped steeply from the abbey and followed a tortuous route into the town. From there, they made their colourful way through the narrow streets, their ever-tinkling bells marking their journey. They were an attraction among the cars and holiday-makers with their doleful faces, decorated harnesses and their names emblazoned across their foreheads. Their steady progress accompanied by the clip-clop of their dainty hooves brought the town's traffic to a slow grind behind them as they were cheered along their route, usually with a procession of happy children prancing around them. Children would sometimes run ahead to their pitch on the yellow sands and make their bids for the first ride on Blossom, Snowdrop, Daffodil or whichever donkey attracted them.

Throughout the long summer days on the beach, the donkeys would stand in an orderly and silent group, regularly carrying happy children or sometimes a giggling adult along the beach and back again for 3d a ride. And then, as evening fell, the tired little troupe would make its return journey through the busy streets for a night's rest.

The lady in charge of them, a dour woman in her sixties, seldom spoke as she ushered them along their daily route through the town; sometimes her grandchildren would accompany her and sometimes her husband, but the donkeys were hers. She owned them, she paid for their upkeep, and she took their earnings as her living.

Within the purple moors which surrounded the town, and indeed within the town itself, there was, and still is, a good deal of folklore surrounding the donkey. For example, there is a legend that suggests no one has ever seen a dead donkey. This is one of those enduring folk beliefs, just as the dark cross on a donkey's back is a reminder that this humble beast carried Christ into Jerusalem on Palm Sunday. And deep in the moors there lingered, until comparatively recent times, a belief that by riding a donkey many cures could be effected, and that the hairs from the cross on its back possessed curative powers. If those hairs were carried in a little bag around the neck of an ailing person, they would prevent toothache, whooping cough and other diseases.

I thought that such superstitions had long disappeared until early one morning, about five o'clock, when I was completing the final hour of a night shift. I was making a last check of lock-up properties along the harbourside when I became aware of an elderly lady walking towards the beach.

She was leading a donkey by its bridle. Seated on the donkey was a girl about nine or ten years of age.

The lady, thick-set with grey hair and a rather handsome, albeit swarthy face, walked with what can be described as a grim determination while the donkey plodded at her heels. This was not the usual donkey lady, although I was sure the animal was one of hers. The colourful harness and tinkling bell suggested that. I watched from the recesses of a yard as the little group moved along the deserted streets towards the sands, and I must admit I was puzzled.

There seemed to be no obvious reason for this, and so, acting on my suspicions, I decided the lady might have stolen the donkey, or removed it from its enclosure for spite or to donate it to the child or for some underhand reason. Clearly it was my duty to clarify the matter, so I stepped out of the darkness of the yard and began to walk along the street as lady and donkey drew alongside me.

'Morning,' I said.

'Now then,' it was evident she did not want company, for her pace increased.

'You're out early?' I began to probe in what I hoped was not an aggressive manner.

'Aye,' she said, tugging at the reins.

'Your donkey, is it?'

'No,' she said, then after a pause, added. 'But Ah've not pinched it, if that's what you're thinking. Ah've got it on a loan, just for this morning.'

'Is it a riding lesson then?' I smiled at the child who sat on board in what did not look to be a very comfortable position.

'No,' she gave another of her short answers.

We walked in silence for a few yards, and I began to wonder about this mission. Her demeanour and her personality assured me that she was not doing anything illegal. I began to wonder how next to question her without appearing too nosy or obnoxious, for there was clearly something curious afoot.

Now that I could look more closely at the lady, I recalled seeing her about the fishmarket from time to time and felt she was the wife of one of the fishermen.

'I've seen you about the fishmarket, haven't I?' I added. 'Gutting herrings and things? Packing ice-boxes?'

'Aye,' she said.

Then the little girl piped up. 'We're off to t'sands. Grandma's going to get me cured,' she said. 'Ah might catch t'mezzles.'

'Oh?' I knew that this was the local dialect word for measles and became more interested now. 'And how are you getting cured?'

The lady spoke again. 'In t'way that's been used hereabouts for years,' she said gruffly. 'Wi' donkey rides and donkey hairs.'

It was then that I recalled the ancient beliefs and was amazed that they should still be regarded as efficacious. I decided not to press the matter any more, and said, 'Well, I hope it works,' and veered away from them.

Ten minutes later, I was walking along the cliff top above the spa buildings and could see the deserted beach, the stretch near the water being as smooth as a plate due to the action of the ebbing tide. And there, approaching the water's edge, was the donkey as it went about its curious mission.

I saw the lady halt it and help the child dismount, and then she executed a rapid action which I knew to be the pulling of three hairs from the donkey's back. She took them from the dark markings of the cross, then took a small bag on a string from her pocket. She placed the hairs inside and fastened the bag around the child's neck. The little girl was replaced in the saddle but facing the donkey's tail, and then the donkey was led up and down the beach on a set route, its feet making deep indentations in the wet sand.

I counted nine trips along the little route, and then the girl was replaced in the more acceptable position, and the donkey was led away. They vanished out of my sight under the cliff.

As I booked off at six o'clock, I asked one of the married officers, 'Is there measles about in the town?'

'Yes,' he acknowledged. 'Why do you ask?'

'Oh, just something I heard,' I said.

It would be three weeks later when I was patrolling in the vicinity of the fishmarket and spotted the lady among a group of women who were gutting fish.

'Hello,' I said, and she nodded in recognition. I watched her deft hands work with the knife she was wielding among the plethora of fish, fish scales and innards, and then asked, 'Did your little girl get the measles?'

'Course not!' she said.

6

A second Adam to the fight,
And to the rescue came.

John Henry, Cardinal Newman 1801–90

The coastal constable requires an ability to remain calm when all around are flapping, and to effect dramatic rescues at a moment's notice. Holiday-makers and indeed local residents possess a remarkable ability to get themselves into some dreadful and highly unlikely situations, and the successful resolution of those situations often requires the expertise of many people with bags of common sense, and some with formal training.

In the short time I was at Strensford, I was staggered by the frequency of incidents which required a rescue team. People of all ages would be cut off by the tide, which meant they had to be hauled up the cliffs on ropes – there were no available helicopters in those days. This occurred time and time again in spite of warnings in the papers and on notice-boards at regular points along the beach. Others would allow themselves to be swept out to sea on dinghies or rubber rafts, some would get lost on the moors behind the town, which meant a fully equipped moorland search party had to range across the hills, and little children would inevitably become separated from their mothers, which meant another type of search party. This one usually consisted of a distraught mother and a solitary constable on tour among the town's ice-cream kiosks and bucket-and-spade shops.

81

Some visitors put themselves beyond the stage of a rescue attempt. It was sobering to learn of the number of suicides along the coast, so often those of people from afar who came to the rugged Strensford coastline especially to throw themselves off the picturesque cliffs. It provided a spectacular finale to an otherwise boring and miserable life, but as a means of solving life's problems it was thoughtless, because it meant someone else had to clear up the mess. It was usually the police who found themselves with that job, although even they would admit it was a highly effective ending for those who took the plunge.

Very few survived those lofty crashes onto jagged rocks; even if they did survive the fall, the raging sea was often on hand to finish the job. Any rescue attempt here usually ended with a dead body rather than a living person. Some determined individuals drove off the cliffs in their cars, and shot themselves in the driving seat as the rolling car trundled towards the edge of the precipice and oblivion.

Over the course of an average summer, therefore, the local police often reached the stage where rescues became so commonplace that they rarely justified comment over a cup of tea. But some were different: some were worth repeating in the pubs and clubs, and in police canteens.

Such was the one which involved County Councillor James L. Whitburn JP, a man of business in the town. An important man, in other words, and particularly so in his own estimation.

Only some five feet two inches tall, Whitburn was a round, fat little man with no hair and not a very handsome face. He had piggy little eyes and a painful high-pitched voice which utterly failed to generate any warmth no matter how hard he tried. He was quite generous to the town, however, although cynical policemen did wonder if he was trying to buy friendship and favour with a view to earning an honour from the Queen. So far as I know, he never got one.

In spite of his unfriendly appearance, he was a successful businessman with a string of shops and businesses in and around Strensford. He proved himself to be a very able councillor too, fighting for the benefit of Strensford. His opinions and strategy were undoubtedly beneficial for the town, but as a magistrate he was disliked by the police.

Fortunately, he was not chairman of the Strensford Bench. This effectively curtailed most of his anti-police activities, although he always managed to make the police feel uncomfortable while giving their evidence. He would question and question the police officers until they were sick and tired of answering his probing, high-pitched voice, which invariably seemed to doubt the quality and veracity of their evidence or the value of the notes they had taken, the language they had used, the formalities they might not have observed, the motives behind their arrest and so on. He never let up, and his unspoken critisms gained regular Press coverage. His insinuations were clear.

For this reason, no policeman liked to appear before Mr Whitburn, and some said they would rather let a petty villain go free than endure the veiled remarks of this spiteful JP. No one knew why he was so vindictive, but it almost reached the stage where the whole police station decided to test his Jaguar every day or check his insurance or find his car in a position where it created an unnecessary obstruction. They would have dearly liked him to appear before his own court to sample the atmosphere before the Bench rather than sit majestically upon it to utter his pontifications.

But we did nothing of the sort. We grumbled a good deal about him, and most of us steadfastly tried to avoid any sitting of the court when he was on the Bench. That was the only action we took – we tolerated him, but only just.

I think the other magistrates even a got a trifle fed up with his persistent and niggling comments, and on more than one occasion the chairman openly cut him short during his spirited inquisitions.

But we cured him, or rather Joe Tapley cured him.

I was patrolling the West Cliff area of Strensford on a shift known as half-nights, that is from 6 p.m. until 2 a.m., and the time had ticked away until it was almost 1 a.m. PC Joe Tapley, probably the most experienced constable in town, was on the adjoining beat, and I saw his torch flashing from a shop doorway. I left my own beat and walked the length of the street to chat with him.

'Would you like to see something interesting?' he asked as I reached him.

'Of course,' I said, not knowing what he had in mind.

He led me to the edge of the cliff, where we sheltered in the shadows of a fancy-goods and ice-cream kiosk and from where we could peer out across the sea and view almost the full length of the long, curving beach. The moon was full and it was a beautiful night, which meant our visibility was excellent.

'Look down there,' said Joe pointing towards the beach, his finger indicating an area below us and slightly to my right.

I could make out the distinctive shape of a dark-coloured Jaguar car which was parked on the beach not far from the foot of a slipway. The lights were out and there was no sign of activity.

'Councillor Whitburn's car,' Joe almost whispered the words as he spoke in a conspiratorial way. 'Do you notice anything else?'

I peered into the moonlit distance but could not see anything worthy of special interest.

'No,' I had to admit. 'Why? What's happening?'

'The tide,' he said in his soft voice. 'It's coming in, and it comes in very fast where he's parked. In less than half an hour, he'll be up to his hubcaps in salt water.'

'Hadn't we better tell him?' I said, thinking this was what Joe had planned.

'No-o-o,' he grinned. 'At least, not just yet. Let's wait a while. He'll be at it right now with someone's wife. His own wife – a lovely woman by the way – will be sitting at home thinking he's out on business. And there's his attitude to our lads in court, eh? I think he needs a little lesson, Nick, and right now you and I are in a perfect position to see that he gets one.'

Joe advised me to keep off the skyline so that our silhouettes would not be visible from the beach, and we made our way down the cliffside paths until we gained an unobstructed view of the dark car. Even now the creeping water was lapping around the front wheels, but the goings-on inside were still a secret, except that we did discern the occasional movement and gentle creak of top-quality leather upholstery. Whatever they were doing was of sufficient interest to render them unaware that the tide was rising so quickly around them.

'He'll never get that car off the beach!' I hissed at Joe as the water rose to cover the tyres at the bottom of the wheels.

'No,' said Joe.

'It'll get inside, won't it?' I persisted, a few minutes later.

'Mebbe,' he said. 'I'm not sure how water-tight those doors are. But if he's busy on the back seat, he'll never notice, will he? Not for a long time, anyway, not until it swishes around his fat body. See, it's touching the bottom of the hubcaps now.'

'When are we going to tell him?' I asked, somewhat worried by the rapid increase in the depth of the water. It was almost possible to see it rising.

'In a minute or two,' he said, to my relief. 'When the moment's right. I've got it all worked out.'

I reasoned that he knew exactly what he was doing, and we waited for a few more minutes, perhaps ten or so, and by then the water was lapping around the centre of the hubcaps and had reached the lower edges of the doors. The sills were now covered.

'We'll give it two more inches,' he said.

When the water was about two inches above the base of the doors, Joe said, 'Right, now we'll raise the alarm.'

With me following tight behind, Joe hurried down the final yards of the path from where we had been waiting, and we came to a halt on the concrete slope of the slipway, right on the edge of the incoming tide. We could go no further because the water was lapping the foot of the slipway. From that point, Joe began to shine his torch on the windows of the silent car, simultaneously shouting and waving the torch about. I did likewise. We made a useful noise and created something of an illuminated commotion.

Our shouts and light-waving precipitated a great deal of action within the car: the wandering beams of our powerful torches touched upon startled eyes, white faces and many flabby lumps of bare flesh as the car rocked with their frantic attempts to adjust or replace their clothing. During that burst of instant action, the expensive leather groaned even more, and the car rocked in its large puddle.

Then the rear door burst open and Councillor Whitburn's piggy little face appeared; he opened his mouth to bawl his displeasure at us but almost immediately found himself standing knee-deep in cold sea-water. This effectively halted his outburst.

'It's the police!' shouted Joe as if we had just arrived in the nick of time. 'You're up to the axles in water . . .'

'Help!' screamed a woman's voice from inside. 'Jim, you'll have to do something . . . Get this car moving, for God's sake . . .'

'You'll never drive it out!' bellowed Joe as the Councillor paddled about in the water, hurrying around to the driving seat. 'Leave it, and come up here.'

'I can't leave it here!' came the squeaky reply. 'I'll drive it out, I'll move it.'

'I'm going!' said the woman. 'This is too bloody embarrassing for words. I'll have you for this, Jim Whitburn!' she cried at him as she disembarked. 'I'll never let you forget this . . . How bloody silly can you get . . .'

She paddled through the swirling water, holding her shoes and stockings high above her head and her skirts almost as high as she struck out for dry land. Joe reached out a hand and hauled her up the slipway.

'Hello, Mrs Beckett,' he greeted her. 'Nice night for a bit of courting, eh?'

'He'll never get me down there again, not ever!' she snapped. 'I'm going home.'

Pausing only to slip on her shoes, the lady stomped away up the slope and vanished towards the town.

'Mrs Beckett,' smiled Joe. 'She's a teacher at one of the schools in town. Nice chap, her husband. She's on the council, too, you see; she's doing her bit for the town tonight, in a manner of speaking.'

Meanwhile, Whitburn had managed to start his engine, and the twin exhausts were making the sea bubble behind the marooned Jaguar; it seemed the water had not reached the interior of the engine, and so long as he could keep it running, the power of the exhausts would keep the water at bay, at least temporarily and at least from that part of the vehicle.

But Whitburn's attempts to drive out of the sea were futile. The wheels utterly refused to grip the sandy surface, and as they turned, it sank deeper into the holes it produced. Accompanied by deep gurgling sounds, the engine spluttered to a halt, and Whitburn came splodging ashore.

'Oh, it's Mr Whitburn,' Joe sounded very surprised. 'Won't it budge, sir?'

'It'll be swamped,' cried the distraught man. 'My car, my new bloody car! It'll be covered – it'll be ruined!'

'I'll drag it out for you,' offered Joe. 'Come on, Nick. Quickly, before the car's completely covered up.'

Parked only yards away, close to the lifeboat house, was the tractor which was always on stand-by to winch the lifeboat, or other boats from the sea. Its winching gear was in position on the rear, and Joe had no trouble starting the engine.

'Grab that cable and hook, Nick, and lead it out to Mr Whitburn as I unwind it. He'll take it. There's no need for you to get wet. Ask him to link it around the back axle of his Jag, and we'll haul it out.'

And so we did. In minutes, the car was back on dry land, a little wet on the outside but very wet on the inside. It was a very relieved Mr Whitburn who began to splutter his thanks, as the water sloshed about the floor of his car. The carpets would be ruined.

'Forget it,' said Joe amiably. 'It's all in the course of duty. There's no harm done, is there?'

'You're both very kind,' he managed to say. 'We might have been drowned . . .'

'I trust the newspapers won't get hold of the tale, Mr Whitburn,' smiled Joe, adopting that amiable smile once again. 'You know the sort of thing they'd print – "Local Magistrate in High Tide Love Drama" . . .'

'You won't tell them, will you?' There was a sudden flash of concern across that podgy face. 'I mean, you are not allowed to talk to the Press, are you?' There was more than a hint of menace in that squeaky voice, even in these circumstances.

'Some things are forbidden, Mr Whitburn, things like internal police matters, the secrets of criminal investigations, a person's criminal record, that sort of thing. But, well, brave rescues by policemen always make a good press. But,' and now Joe spoke very slowly. 'I'm sure that if you adopt a more sympathetic approach to our men in court, that you bury whatever grievance you are nursing against my colleagues, then we'll say nowt about this unfortunate little episode. There's only us know about it, and Mrs Beckett, but I reckon she'll not say much.'

It seemed to take a long time for the import of this statement to filter through to his anxious brain, but in time it did and Whitburn said, 'Well, I'm only after the truth, you know, for the sake of justice. We must have the truth in court.'

'Precisely,' agreed Joe.

'I'll try to listen more carefully,' promised the unhappy Whitburn as he thanked us again and then went to examine his dripping Jaguar. We left him to his worries and together strolled contentedly back to the police station.

'I think we should have got him out earlier,' I said with a twinge of conscience. 'We could have saved his car from damage.'

'Nick, young man,' said Joe. 'That old bastard could have ruined a good marriage, that teacher I mean, Mrs Beckett. She's a good woman, but silly to get tangled up with him. I reckon I've saved that marriage tonight, I might even have saved Whitburn's own marriage too, I've certainly done something to uphold the good name of the magistracy by keeping a scandal out of the papers – imagine what would have been said if they had drowned, and both of them in the nude too! And I've done our lads a little service as well. And the cost? Well, there's some embarrassment to Whitburn and Mrs Beckett, and a spot of sea-water damage to an expensive car. It'll always have a salt-water tide-mark round it from now on, as a small reminder of his experience. In all, I'd say he's learned a lesson, and for everyone it was a bargain, well worth the price.'

We arrived back at the station at 2 a.m. Sergeant Blaketon was the duty sergeant and asked, 'Well, Rhea? Tapley? Is everything correct on your beats?'

'All correct, sergeant,' we assured him.

Oddly enough, Joe Tapley and I were involved in another, more dramatic rescue from the sea, and it occurred within yards of the place where Whitburn's car had floundered. On this second occasion, some three weeks after the car incident, I was patrolling a night shift and had taken a long stroll along the pier. It was a peaceful, quiet night with a warm August breeze blowing off the land; it was an ideal night for long walks in peaceful contemplation. Indeed, it was pleasant on such a night to be a patrolling policeman; anyone out on a night like this owned the world. There was nothing to interrupt that peace and tranquillity; it was a blessed state which was there to be enjoyed.

Making use of a spare twenty minutes or so just after midnight, I had circumnavigated the lighthouse and had regained the streets of the town. I was waiting near the circular bandstand about half-past midnight because I knew Joe would pass this way *en route* to his next point. We made use of such meetings for brief chats, always a welcome respite during a lonely night patrol, and so I stood beside the bandstand, waiting in the warm night air.

I could see Joe's distinctive, rather ambling figure moving steadily towards me down the winding slopes of Captain's Pass, and as I watched him, I became aware of a young couple, a man and woman in their early twenties, racing towards me with their arms waving and shouting with enough fervour to rouse the whole town.

Joe had obviously heard them too, because he started to run towards them at the same time as I, and we all arrived together at the top of one of the concrete slipways. The couple were panting heavily, and I saw that their feet were bare, wet and sandy – obviously they'd just raced up from the beach. It was some time before they could pant out their news.

'Take it calmly,' said Joe, always a sobering influence. 'Easy now. Get your breath back.'

The man was pointing to the sea; we could hear the regular slap of the waves in the darkness beside the pier, just down the slipway behind us.

'Man, down there. Drowning . . . we tried to get him . . .'

'Right!' and with that Joe darted off with me in hot pursuit. He didn't wait for anything further but took immediate action. We raced onto the wet sands, and as we left the streets and houses of the town, the darkness hit us. We used our torches but the movement of the sea and our own rushing footsteps made it difficult to see anything in the bobbing lights. The couple had caught up to us, and the man was pointing.

'About here,' he said. 'In the sea. He waded in, fully dressed. I tried to stop him, but he hit me and said he was going to end it all.'

'When?' asked Joe.

'Just now, minutes before I found you. We could make nothing of him . . .'

'Jerry tried to drag him out,' panted the girl.

'Is he a local chap, then?' asked Joe.

'Dunno,' said the man called Jerry. 'I'm not. We're on holiday.'

As we talked, we ranged the circular glow of our torches across the sea, and then the beach, and then the sea again, but saw nothing. I began to wonder if we were too late, if the fellow, whoever he was, had gone under the surface for ever. The sea was well out; the tide was turning and would soon sweep in across those bare sands.

I lifted my own torch and searched the waves further out. Only a matter of yards from the shoreline, they rolled in majestically before breaking and roared up the beach. And there, suddenly, I caught sight of him. My beam reflected upon his wet clothing and hair, creating a momentary burst of brilliance out there in the wet darkness, and so I shouted and held my light on him. He was attempting to wade out in the face of the incoming waves; they were making his progress difficult as he breasted each new wave, the strength of it lifting him onto his toes as he fought to make progress.

There were no boats here, save the lifeboat tucked away in its shed, and there was no time to raise its crew; thinking as one person, Joe and I threw off our jackets and caps and waded in. We passed our torches to the young couple, asking them to keep the twin beams on the figure ahead of us. They would have to be our guides in the darkness.

'Don't shout,' said Joe. 'Just wade like hell.'

But it was easier said than done. When the sea was higher than our knees, we found the going very tough, but we forged ahead; sometimes the fellow would stop as if contemplating his fate, and this allowed us to gain a few precious feet, but in no time the water was up to our waists.

'We can't hang about too long,' said Joe. 'The tide's coming in. Come on, he's not far off now.'

The man, with the sea up to his chest, was finding the going more difficult than we did, but as it rose to our chests we had the same trouble. Then, with a terrible cry, he fell headlong into the water, arms outstretched; the torch beams shone into the unseen distance, and for a moment or two we lost him.

'Keep them shining near us!' bellowed Joe, and so we began to hunt for him among the rise and fall of the incoming tide.

'There!' I had seen him, floating face down apparently determined to drown himself, even if his clothing and the air in his lungs kept him afloat. He wore a fawn mackintosh which floated around him, making him fairly visible in the dark water.

The action of the incoming tide carried him closer to us as we waded out, and this helped us to reach him. The light of the torches was bobbing about close to us and helped a little. Without speaking, Joe and I separated as we closed in, and each of us seized an arm and lifted the man out of the water. He struggled in our grasp, coughing and spluttering, but we knew how to contain a person and in no time had our arms tight under his so that we could walk out of the sea, with him trailing behind and moving backwards towards dry land.

We carried him high onto the beach and laid him gently down. He was now silent. The couple came closer and shone torches on him. He was a very thin person, a man about forty with a head of lank, black hair and very white face. He wore a suit under his old raincoat, and a white shirt and black tie.

Joe slapped his face.

'Leave me alone. I want to die,' he said. 'I just want to die . . .'

'That's not allowed,' said Joe. 'At least, not while we're about. So, you're not dead yet, which means we'll take you to hospital. Come on, on your feet.'

The man just lay there, so we turned to the couple to obtain their names and address, for we'd probably need a statement from them about the affair. Then we went off to locate our hats and jackets.

But in those few seconds, the man had leapt to his feet and was running back into the waves.

'Bloody hell, you can't turn your backs for a minute!' shouted Joe. 'Come on, Nick, here we go again.'

In those few moments the determined self-destructor had gained ten or twenty yards on us, and by the time we had thrown our belongings back to the ground and shouted for the couple to shine their torches upon him once again, he had reached the water. By the time we caught him, he was up to his waist in strong sea-water, thrashing ahead with enormous splashes as if he intended wading across the entire North Sea.

This time we caught him before he had time to lie down in the water, and we executed the same move as previously. But this time it didn't work. He began to thrash his arms and simultaneously kicked, shouted and struggled; he became like a human dynamo and windmill combined as he created a huge maelstrom in the water. In spite of this, we did manage to haul him to the shore, although both Joe and I got several knocks to our faces and bruises about our wet bodies. It was exhausting work.

As we arrived on the beach, he fell to the ground rather like a child who does not want to go for a walk, so we drew him along the sand and laid him down once more. He lay like a saturated rag doll.

'Let me die,' he was sobbing now. 'I just want to die. Why can't I die if I want to?'

Joe addressed the young man who was still hovering about with Joe's police torch shining upon the saturated fellow.

'Jerry,' Joe had remembered the man's name. 'Be a good chap and call an ambulance, will you? There's a kiosk near the bandstand, where you found us, and the hospital's number is 2277. Tell them to come to the West Pier, and you wait there until they do, then call us.'

Jerry ran off to perform this useful task, while we and the girl stood around as the would-be suicide lay on the beach, weeping and covering his face with his sandy hands. We stood close enough to prevent him from another sprint into the waves. The girl, now shivering violently, stood at a discreet distance with her teeth chattering.

'What will happen to him?' she asked, with obvious concern in her voice.

'We'll get him to hospital,' said Joe. 'They'll see to him. I would imagine he'll come back to his senses after a day or so.'

'I'm pleased you rescued him,' she smiled, holding a cardigan tight about her slender body.

'He owes his life to you,' I said. 'You noticed him and did something about it – promptly too.'

The man was struggling to get to his feet, and we were very wary of his next move. Already, I could feel the beginning of a black eye from his earlier thrash, and as I helped him to his feet I was very aware that he might attempt a new trick. But he didn't. He stood beside us, dripping wet with his head hung low.

'What's your name?' Joe asked him.

'I'm not saying. I'm not saying anything,' was his reply.

'Suit yourself,' said Joe. And so we waited in silence and then, after about five long minutes, Jerry returned, waving the torch once again.

'It's come,' he called. 'The ambulance, it's waiting at the top of the slipway.'

'Come on,' Joe took the man's arm, but in a flash he had shaken free and was once more sprinting like a gazelle across the beach, heading for the crashing waves.

'This joker does not give up!' and with a cry, Joe and I set off in hot pursuit.

This time we reached him before he gained the water, and although I do not claim to be a Rugby football player, I did launch myself at him in what could be described as a flying tackle. I brought him down among cascades of sand only feet from the water's edge, and he promptly began another fierce and powerful struggle, with Joe and me battling for control. This time, it was a fierce and bloody fight. I got a bloody nose from a flailing fist, Joe had a tooth loosened, but it seemed impossible to subdue this man whose insane strength appeared to grow greater as ours weakened.

It was like fighting with a whirlwind; his crazy mind seemed to have driven him berserk, and as we fought on that beach, he was just as determined to drown himself as we were to stop him.

It was Joe who stopped him. With a mighty blow to the man's stomach, Joe winded him, and as he doubled up in breathless agony, Joe delivered a punch which would have delighted any boxer. It caught the man on the chin, and it felled him.

'Sorry, old son,' said Joe to the unconscious man at his feet. 'But we can't mess about all night.'

We carried him to the ambulance, thanked the young couple and walked back to the station to arrange some dry clothing.

The following day, as we paraded for duty, the Inspector was waiting for us at 10 p.m.

'Rhea and Tapley,' he said. 'Report to my office before you go to your beats.'

We went through and stood before his desk, and he joined us soon afterwards. He looked us up and down, then said, 'Would either of you describe yourself as violent?'

Joe and I shook our heads and denied such a possibility.

'Well,' said the Inspector. 'We have received, via the hospital, a complaint against two of my constables. It seems that a patient alleges he was swimming in the sea last night, and was assaulted by two uniformed police officers. Now I know this occurred in the area which formed part of your beat, both your beats, in fact. I need not say that I regard this as a very serious allegation, and I want you both to think very carefully before making any response . . .'

'No comment,' said Joe.

And I concurred.
'Well done, the pair of you,' he smiled.

7

Husbands, love your wives
Be not bitter against them.

St Paul (to the Colossians)

If there is one aspect of human behaviour which stands out more than any other in police work, it is the multitude of ways in which husbands and wives manage to deceive one another. Within the broad range of their miscellaneous duties, observant police officers see and learn much about the way that life is actually lived, rather than the way it appears to be lived, and this marital quirk is constantly observed.

In the area of supposed domestic bliss, therefore, the police are guardians of many secrets. They keep their eyes and ears open but their mouths firmly shut, for they know, often to their cost, that strife between man and wife causes more serious trouble than anything else.

Domestic rows in varying degrees of ferocity are a nightly feature of police work; one spouse engages in noisy and violent battle against the other, often over some trivial matter, and when the neighbours call the police in an attempt to restore order, the warring pair band together to assault the unfortunate peace-keeping constable. So police officers everywhere learn to cope with these outbursts.

Most 'domestics', as we call them, are concluded as rapidly as they arise, although some do spill into the streets as the whole neighbourhood joins the mayhem. Quite often, a good time is had by all.

Problems that arise through a man or wife misbehaving sexually, however, call for a different technique. The fact is noted, possibly for future use, but a discreet silence is maintained, even if the people in question are prominent in local public life. Discretion is an essential quality of police officers. The Yorkshire motto of "Hear all, see all and say nowt" was probably coined by a policeman with a long experience of others' illicit affairs. Every police officer has, at some stage of his or her service, had to cope with a domestic problem of some kind.

It is not often that real love or genuine respect by one spouse for another causes those kind of problems. Usually, it is lack of those virtues which creates the agonies. Yet on two occasions at Strensford, love or respect, or possibly a combination of both, did cause domestic problems in which the police were involved.

The first concerned Mr and Mrs Furnell, Edward and Caroline to their friends. They owned and ran a splendid private hotel on the clifftop; it was a veritable treasure house of style and culture, the sort of place frequented by very discerning visitors with money enough to pay for their expensive and exclusive pleasures. The sheer cost of staying there kept at bay those of lesser quality, and there is no doubt that the genteel luxury of "Furnells", as it was simply known, did establish standards which set it apart from the average seaside hotel.

Edward was a charming man. In his late forties, he was tall and slender, with a head of good, thick black hair which was greying with distinction around the temples. He was always smart in a dark grey suit or a blazer and flannels, and his turn-out was positively immaculate. He was handsome too, with a lean, tanned face and a sensuous walk which attracted many women. But in spite of the opportunities which must have presented themselves, he was never unfaithful to Caroline. Indeed, he was a pillar of the Anglican Church, a very active member of the Parochial Church Council and a sidesman who never missed the Sunday service. He was almost too good to be true as he ran his hotel with scrupulous honesty. Everyone thought he was a perfect specimen of manhood, an example to all. There is no doubt that many people regarded Edward as an example of the ideal husband and businessman, and that many husbands found themselves openly compared with him.

Caroline was similarly well endowed with good looks and charm. If a little inclined to be plump, she did her best to appear smart on every occasion, when her blonde hair would be set in the latest style, her make-up impeccable, her clothing beautiful and her treatment of others charming and welcoming. A little younger than Edward, she would be in her mid-thirties. Although she lived in a world of expensive tastes enjoyed by expensive people, she was neither aloof nor snobbish. At times she was a real bundle of good humour and warmth, especially on those rare occasions when she was not in the austere company of her proud husband.

There were times when I did wonder if Caroline would be more relaxed and 'ordinary' if Edward was not around. In my view, it did seem that his presence sometimes overawed or even suppressed her, and there were times when I wondered if she was trying desperately to live up to his life-style. I felt he set standards which were not normal for her. Marriage to Edward had perhaps forced her to adopt his particular way of life, but she coped admirably and everyone liked her.

The Furnells were always happy, always good company and always an example to others. Patrolling policemen were welcome to pop into their hotel kitchen for a cup of tea and a warm-up on ice-cold mornings. That's how we got to know the couple so well. Our presence served a dual purpose, because if there was any doubt about a guest, we would be told and we would carry out discreet enquiries in case he or she absconded without paying the bill. We had physical descriptions and car numbers well in advance, just in case.

This enviable state of bliss continued until Caroline started driving-lessons. Edward, perfectionist that he was, insisted on teaching his wife, because he felt he could do it so much better than anyone else. This practice is never recommended for normal husbands and wives, for there is no finer way to generate marital problems than to teach one's wife to drive. For some reason, a woman behind a steering wheel will steadfastly refuse to learn anything she is taught by her husband, and she will likewise blame him for all that goes wrong. How many lady drivers, when they have had a minor driving upset, have said to their husbands, 'You made me do that!'

But Edward was not a normal man. He was Mr Perfect, and so he guided his wife around the town's maze of quaint narrow streets, pedestrian crossings, junctions, lanes, bridges and corners and through columns of gawping tourists and dizzy townspeople until she was a very proficient driver. Sometimes they went out very early in the morning and sometimes very late at night for Caroline's lessons, although he did take her into the thick of the daytime traffic whenever his hotel duties permitted.

And Edward, being so particular about things, sent her to a driving school for the finishing touches before she took her test – even he admitted the experts did have a role to play. And then, one day in late August, Caroline was due to take her driving test.

Edward was engaged with a conference of businessmen at the hotel, so Caroline walked the half-mile or so to the testing centre in Strensford, where the driving school's car would be waiting. She said the walk and fresh sea air would calm her nerves before the ordeal.

An hour later, she returned to the hotel, where Edward was waiting.

'Well, darling?' he asked.

'Isn't it wonderful?' she breathed. 'I passed, Edward, I passed. First time! Me, a driver!'

'I knew you would, darling. I just knew. Now, here's a little present for you,' and he handed her an ignition key. Outside, on the car-park of their hotel, stood a brand new Morris 1000 in pale blue.

'It's for you,' he said. 'A present from me.'

And so the citizens, and indeed the police, became accustomed to seeing Caroline chugging around in her lovely little car, sometimes shopping, sometimes going about hotel business or merely visiting friends.

Then, one busy morning in early September, something went wrong. No one is quite sure what happened, but the little car ran out of control down Captain's Pass with a panicking Caroline at the wheel. She collided with some iron railings outside a café which acted like a spring, for she bounced off and slewed across the road like a shot from a gun. Having been catapulted across the road in this manner, miraculously missing other cars and wandering pedestrians on its terrifying journey, her little car mounted the opposite footpath and careered across an ornamental garden. It concluded its short but impressive journey among a jumble of rocks, cotoneasters and geraniums. The Council's Parks Department were not very pleased about it.

Fortunately, Caroline was not hurt, although she was rather embarrassed, and the immaculate little car suffered some plants in its radiator grill, a badly dented door panel, buckled wings and other minor abrasions. As a result, the machinery of law began to move, the police were informed and I arrived at the scene.

It was a 'damage only' accident involving just one vehicle, with no personal injuries, so there were few problems. Willing helpers manhandled the car out of the flowerbed, and it was still driveable; meanwhile, the shaken Caroline was muttering something about a black dog running over the road and causing her to lose control.

Having ensured she was not hurt, I had to ask for her driving licence and insurance; she did not have them with her and therefore opted to produce them at Strensford Police Station within the legally stipulated five days. This was standard procedure in such a case. I did not expect any further proceedings, although I had to chant the words of a 'Notice of Intended Prosecution' at her, this being a statutory formality at that time in case there followed a prosecution for careless driving or some other more serious driving offence.

I asked if I should take her home and she declined. She insisted she was fit to drive, and in any case she would like to break the news to Edward herself. So off she went.

I was not at the police station when she arrived to produce her documents but shortly afterwards was summoned to see Sergeant Blaketon.

'Rhea,' he stood before me at his full majestic height. 'This Mrs Furnell of yours, the accident on Captain's Pass. She's been to produce her documents. You'll have to go and see her – her driving licence is not valid, and this being so, neither is the insurance on that car. It's your case, so you'll have to follow it up.'

When I looked at the details of her licence in the Production of Documents Book, they were for her provisional one, which had expired, albeit only a week earlier.

'She's probably brought the wrong one in,' said Sergeant Blaketon. 'Go and sort it out.'

When I arrived at Furnells, Caroline was not her normal, immaculate self. She was alone in the office as Edward attended to some business at the Bank, and she gave me a coffee. But she was paler than usual, her lovely eyes looked dark and sad, her hair much less tidy than normal and her general demeanour much less confident.

'I know why you're here,' she looked steadily into my eyes. 'I'm sorry.'

'You produced an out-of-date licence,' I said, probably unnecessarily. 'It was your old provisional one. I need the new one, the one that was valid on the date of your accident. If it was a provisional one too, I'll need the driving examiner's slip to confirm that you passed your test, or, of course, I'll need a full licence.'

She hung her head.

'I didn't. I failed,' she said slowly. 'I failed that bloody driving test, officer! And I daren't tell that perfect bloody husband of mine! I daren't tell him I was a failure! He does not recognize anything that's second rate, he can't tolerate anything that's a failure, so I told him I'd passed. And when I said I'd passed, he gave me that car – it was all ready and waiting for me. He never thought I'd fail, you see. Never. So what could I do? I daren't tell him, not after all that.' She was weeping now. 'So I got myself into a trap . . . a snobby, awfully stupid trap. I don't know what he'll say when I tell him.'

She wiped her eyes, and her make-up began to run down her cheeks. She looked anything but elegant and self-assured.

'He doesn't know? Not even about the accident?' I was incredulous.

'No. I got the car fixed – it wasn't damaged much . . . but this will get my name in the papers, won't it? He'll have to know now, won't he?'

'It depends. You see, if you've no provisional licence in force, it could mean your insurance is automatically invalid too. And you were driving unaccompanied by a qualified driver. And you had no "L" plates on. There's a lot of offences, Mrs Furnell. I've got to report you for them all.'

I had to go through all the formalities of notifying her of an impending prosecution for those offences and possibly a 'careless driving', but the decision about a prosecution was not mine. Ultimately, it rested with the Superintendent, who would study my report and make up his mind from the facts which I presented.

A few days later, I did see her driving around town again, with 'L' plates up and with a driving instructor at her side. She waved as she passed me. But I had finished my tour of duty at Strensford before she appeared at court.

I do not know what fate she suffered before the magistrates, although it would probably involve a fine of some kind with endorsement of her new licence for the insurance offence. I do not know how Edward accepted this blemish to his reputation, but I like to think that he, being a perfect gentleman, had treated his unhappy wife like a perfect lady.

The other case was very similar. It happened because Nathan Fleming loved his wife so much that he kept a guilty secret from her.

I had frequently seen Nathan about town because he was one of those characters that everyone knows, likes and respects. He seemed to be everywhere, a truly ubiquitous character. He was a member of one of Strensford's oldest fishing families and owned several fishing boats which plied from the town's picturesque harbour. In addition, he had a couple of wet fish-shops, a whelk stall and a little van which toured the outer regions of the town on Tuesdays, Thursdays and Saturdays.

I was never sure of his age. He was one of those men who could have been anything between forty-five and sixty, a stocky, powerful man with the swarthy, dark features of the indigenous fisherfolk. More often than not, he had a few days' growth of whiskers on his chin, and when about town he invariably wore a dark blue ganser with a high neck, even in the height of summer, along with blue overalls and heavy rubber seaboots. The ganser's name is a corruption of guernsey, the name for a thick, dark-blue woollen jumper which originated in Guernsey on the Channel Islands. A jersey comes from Jersey too. Those boots came up to his thighs when on the boat, but he rolled them down when not on the boat, so that when he walked he looked like a tiny man in a pair of giant seven-league boots.

A distinctive aura surrounds a Strensford fisherman. It is difficult to define but doubtless comes from centuries of extremely tough work in appalling conditions on the North Sea. His clothes are sensible and ideal for the task, if almost a uniform; his skin and face are hard, weather-beaten and tanned; his language is also hard and liberally spiced with a dialect all of his own, a dialect that even his colleagues from Scandinavia can understand.

These fishermen live in a closed community, their familes having lived and worked here since Viking times. It is rare, indeed very rare, for them to marry outside their own kind.

That is why Nathan's wife was so different. She was not from a Strensford fishing family but hailed from the Midlands. It seems she and Nathan had met as young people when she came to Strensford for a holiday, and much to everyone's surprise they married. She became the brains behind his various business enterprises, but she was not like the wives of the other fishermen.

Those other wives had emerged from days, fairly recent days, when the women virtually lived on the fish quays, drying the fish in the open in summer, gutting crans of herring and stones of cod, packing them in large ice-boxes, mending nets and baiting lines in spite of the weather and in spite of the hour. Being a fisherman's wife was hard, very hard.

Laura Fleming had had none of those experiences. She'd been reared near the Trent, the daughter of a shopkeeper in Stoke, and she had no intention of sitting all day among stinking fish and their bloody innards. So, by her own conduct, she was a woman apart, but a thoroughly decent woman who became a loved and respected member of Strensford society. She was President of the Townswomen's Guild, a strong Methodist and sincere chapel-goer as well as a tireless worker for charity.

I'd seen her once or twice. I'd noticed her supervising the assistants in their shops or at the summer-time whelk stall. She was a smart woman in middle age who enjoyed a light, peachy complexion which was such a contrast against the dark ruggedness of the other fisherfolk. Her features alone marked her out as a stranger among the local people, and her uncharacteristic mode of speech was another difference. Her mousy hair, just turning grey when I knew her, was always tightly tied in a bun, and she always wore sensible shoes, thick stockings and clothes which concealed her figure. Like Nathan, she was always busy with something, either running the shops, raising money for worthwhile causes, such as the Royal National Lifeboat Institution or various other maritime charities, or going about chapel business.

Being a policeman means that it is possible to acquire a knowledge of people without even realizing it; as citizens like Laura go about their daily routine, and as the policeman does likewise, their paths cross, they chat and they begin to discover more and more about one another, albeit unintentionally. Gossip, parade-room chat and frequent talks with my Strensford colleagues all provided little snippets about Nathan and Laura which I stored in my memory, usually subconsciously. It was all part of local knowledge, such an asset in police work.

The other fishermen's wives accepted Laura; there was no antagonism, and this may have had something to do with the fact that she was the wife of the respected Nathan Fleming, or it could have been due to Laura's own personality and quiet charm. Or a combination of both.

But it was Nathan I saw more than his wife. When he was not on his boat or seeing to his whelk stall, he was driving his van around the outskirts, pulling up in the streets as his customers flocked to buy what he described as the freshest fish in town. Whenever he stopped near me, I would gaze in admiration as he wielded his knife to provide every customer with a choice piece of the right weight, and he always found a morsel for the cats which rubbed their chins against his van wheels during these sales.

There were times when I wondered when he slept or took a break from his fishing and the business it generated. He was always busy, always to be seen around town, always happy and pleasant with people, always making a pound or two here and a shilling or two there. He did not run a car, so I wondered how he spent his hard-earned cash, although his home was beautiful. It was a large, old house which his wife, with her tasteful talents, had decorated and renovated, but I wondered when he found the time to enjoy it.

He did employ others though; sometimes a young man would serve at the whelk stall, or wheel barrow-loads of fresh fish from the quay to the shops, or drive the van because Nathan was at sea. But the moment he returned, he did those tasks himself, apparently tirelessly.

As policemen are prone to do simply by keeping their ears and eyes open, I did learn what Nathan had secretly done with some of his hard-earned money. He did a lot of cash dealing, and over the years he had managed to siphon off a considerable amount of money. This had accumulated to such an extent that he had difficulty knowing what to do with it. To spend it on new equipment or a new business venture might exercise the curiosity of HM Inland Revenue who could begin to ask awkward questions. Worse still, I learned, was that he had managed to accumulate this nest-egg without the knowledge of his dear Laura. That alone suggested cunning of a very high standard.

According to tales which were circulating the police station, through Joe Tapley's intimate knowledge of the fisherfolk, Nathan had kept his growing wad of cash on his boat. It had been concealed from everyone behind a clever piece of panelling, but the time had come, several months before my arrival in Strensford, for Nathan to do something about it. There was too much even for the place of concealment so he had either to confess to its presence and spend it on the business or bank it, every action being likely to arouse official scrutiny of his income.

The other alternative was to buy something expensive, such as an oil painting or piece of furniture, but that would cause Laura to ask too many questions. Besides, he wasn't one for admiring paintings or acquiring furnishings of excess quality.

So he bought a racehorse.

Very few people knew about this acquisition; it was a very odd thing to do because Nathan had never shown any interest in either horses or racing. We did wonder if it was done upon the advice of another businessman, the logic being that horse-racing, especially betting on the outcome, is one of the finest and speediest ways of getting rid of money.

Joe Tapley was one of the few people who knew of Nathan's purchase, and I know he did not spread the news indiscriminately. Nonetheless, he did tell me during one of our lone patrols, and he provided me with the history of Nathan which I have just related. This revelation and life history were prompted when we saw Nathan hurrying to his boat at 3.30 one morning.

Joe told me the horse was called Beggar's Bridge because it had nothing to do with fish.

'Has it won much?' I asked, not being a racing fan and therefore not knowing the reputation of this animal.

'It hasn't raced yet,' he said. 'It's due for its first outing later this year.'

'There'll be a lot of local interest in it,' I said almost as an aside. 'The whole town will be backing it, surely?'

'They won't!' said Joe. 'No one knows it's Nathan's, not even his wife. He hasn't told her.'

'You're joking!' I cried. 'Surely he's told his wife? I mean, it'll cost a bomb to train and keep . . .'

'He can't tell her, can he? She'll ask where he got the money to buy it and train it. Besides, she's a big chapel lady and doesn't hold with gambling. God knows what she'd do if she discovered Nathan owned a racehorse! Nathan will never tell her, Nick. So the fewer folks know about it, the better, then she's not likely to find out, is she?'

I knew that the code among Nathan's men friends would

never allow Laura to learn of her husband's investment, but it seemed inevitable that one day she would learn from someone else about Nathan's secret racehorse.

I thought no more about it until one Saturday in late July. It was a warm, bright day with dark clouds scudding across the sky, interspersed with periods of intense sunshine, so typical of the month. I was working a beat just out of the town centre where I had to supervise the indiscriminate parking of cars by visitors and day trippers. My job was to ensure that all the coaches were left in the official parks provided by the Urban District Council.

This was before the days of yellow 'No Parking' lines and traffic wardens, and one major problem was that thoughtless drivers would park all day in the side streets and so block entrances to the homes of the local people. Even shops and other business premises found themselves blocked in with parked cars. We tried to solve the problem by positioning 'No Parking' signs at frequent intervals, but some motorists would move the signs so they could park their cars! We hit back by booking them for 'Unnecessary obstruction of the highway', but often they had dumped their cars and departed before we could catch them. In those days we did not tow cars away to compounds, and so the poor townspeople often had to tolerate this gross inconvenience. It was a constant battle – the motorists thought we were harassing them, and the locals thought we were doing too little about them.

Over my lunch of salad sandwiches and coffee in the muster room of Strensford's ancient police station that Saturday, Joe Tapley was chattering as usual, and I was listening to his fund of local yarns.

'Well,' he said eventually. 'Who's having five bob on Beggar's Bridge today? It's in the 3.15 at Thirsk.'

I pricked up my ears. This was Nathan's horse, but how many of the men knew that? I kept quiet but said to Joe, 'I wouldn't mind having a crack at it. What's the price?'

'I can get seven to one,' he said. 'I've a friend who can place any bets for us.'

I passed over my two half-crowns and made a silent wish that

Beggar's Bridge would carry them safely home at a profit. And having done that, I left the station and returned to the chore of instructing irate motorists to move their cars.

I had no doubt that when I returned to my beat after lunch, there would be several illegally and stupidly parked vehicles, and that I would spend hours hopelessly trying to find the drivers. We had a pad of tickets for such cases, so I could always stick one of them in each offending windscreen, asking the driver to call at the police office to explain why he had parked in a 'No Parking' street.

It was while patrolling one of the Georgian crescents on the West Cliff that I found a car very badly parked outside a boarding house. I decided to locate the driver by asking inside one or more of those boarding houses. After only two attempts, I entered one called Sea Vista and found the landlady in her little kitchen. She was watching television and, as I put my request about the badly parked car, I automatically looked at my watch. It was ten past three – I needed a note of the time if I was to book an offender.

The man, it seemed, was staying at Sea Vista and had just registered; he was upstairs now, having lugged suitcases and bags up several flights, and so I asked her to request him to move it the moment he had unloaded. I went outside and he appeared within seconds, flustered and full of apologies, so I directed him to a convenient car-park and decided not to report him for a prosecution. I had no intention of spoiling his holiday, for he was clearly a genuine fellow doing his best for a growing family.

The moment he'd vacated the space, Nathan's fish van rushed into the crescent and halted in the very same spot. Out he leapt and, instead of opening his van doors, he hurried to the door of Sea Vista, knocked and rushed inside. I wondered if there was an emergency, and so, thinking the car-parking episode would give me an excuse for going back, I followed.

'Mrs Parkin,' I hard Nathan say. 'Can I see your telly? Tyne-Tees? Sports.'

'Well, Nathan, I was waiting to get my order, but . . .'

The set was already on and tuned into the sports programme,

and when she saw me hovering she said, 'Dunno what he wants, but it must be interesting. Your man moved his car, has he?'

'Thanks, yes,' I said, and then it dawned on me! The 3.15 at Thirsk.

'Can I watch as well?' I asked her. 'I've a little bet on Beggar's Bridge. It's running now, 3.15.'

'So have I. One of my guests said it was a good bet. Come in both of you. It's due to start.'

As the horses went to the start, she offered us a cup of tea from the ever-singing kettle, and by the time they reached the start we were all settled in silence before her TV set, the parking regulations forgotten.

Beggar's Bridge was No. 8, which showed up clearly on the black-and-white screen, and we all sat in total silence as the starter's flag went up. Then they were off. Nathan started shouting 'Come on, come on,' and I found myself watching him as much as I was watching the race.

In seconds it was all over. Nathan's horse had won by three lengths. It was a good, substantial win. As Beggar's Bridge crossed the line, Nathan leapt out of his chair, hugged Mrs Parkin and gave her a huge, smacking kiss, then rushed outside and came back with her order.

'Mrs Parkin,' he said with tears of joy streaming down his weathered cheeks. 'You've made me a very happy man today. Take this fish as a gift, a memento of today. I love everybody!'

She was lost for words and looked at me in total amazement.

'What got into him?' she gasped.

'I don't know,' I smiled, and after thanking her too, I followed him down the steps and out to his van. He had closed the doors and was walking round to the driving seat as I arrived.

'Well done,' I said.

He studied me for a few moments and then smiled a long, slow smile.

'You had something on him, then?'

'Five bob,' I said.

'Good,' and he prepared to drive away.

'You didn't go to Thirsk to watch it run?' I put to him.

'How could I?' He shrugged his shoulders. 'What could I tell Laura?'

'What can you tell her now?' I countered.

'Search me,' he said.

'You've another problem looming as well, you know,' I whispered to him, man to man.

'What's that?' There was a genuine look of curiosity on his happy face.

'Mrs Parkin,' I said, indicating her bow window with a sideways nod of my head. She was gazing out at him, and there was the fire of love and longing in her eyes. 'How are you going to cope with her next week?'

8

The man's desire is for the woman.

Samuel Taylor Coleridge, 1772–1834

A heady summer-time mixture of sunshine, sea, fresh air and freedom invariably gives rise to nature's desires among healthy young people. That summer at Strensford also affected healthy older people. Perhaps it was the sight of bikini-clad beauties reclining on the sands that provided the necessary stimulus for the older chaps. But whatever the cause, it certainly brought more than a sparkle to their eyes because their wives seemed to spend all their time cooling down their husbands' obvious ardour instead of nurturing it for their own enjoyment.

Perhaps they knew that any nurtured love would not be channelled in their direction? The sexual adventures of the mature British male are fairly well documented in books, magazines, the *News of the World* and the divorce courts, so it is perhaps wise for middle-aged wives to keep a tight rein on their holidaying middle-aged husbands. Memories of a rampant youthfulness can be dangerous in advancing years. St Matthew summed it up succinctly when he said, 'The spirit is indeed willing, but the flesh is weak.'

During my early constabulary years, it was not considered seemly for young ladies to make overtures to young men, at least not in a way they would be noticed, although it must be stressed that, so far as cleverness and cunning are concerned in the eternal search for love (even if it is for a mere five minutes rather

113

than something earth-shattering and eternal), the female sex leaves the masculine far behind.

For all, therefore, whether young or old, male or female, a holiday at the seaside is like a second spring. There, a young man's fancy lightly turns to thoughts of young women, and an older man's fancy heavily turns to thoughts of older women, middle-aged women and younger women. In those days, it was not considered normal for a young man's fancy lightly to turn to thoughts of other young men; consequently, when such thoughts developed into positive action, it was very illegal.

For ladies to fancy other ladies, however, and then to take practical steps to achieve their desires, was not unlawful. This was due not to the efforts of early feminists but to Queen Victoria. I have been assured that when a statute, which would have outlawed lesbianism, was presented to Her Majesty for the necessary royal signature, she refused to believe that such disgraceful things happened and promptly crossed out the relative sections of the Act. Thus lesbians won some kind of privilege – which to this day they still enjoy in spite of apparent sexual equality.

When faced with a seaside resort full of randy young men and available young women, the coastal constable had to be very aware of the provisions of the Sexual Offences Act of 1956 which legislated for many curious facets of human behaviour. We learned to recognize prostitutes (purely for future action which might have to be taken in the course of our duty!) and to know what constituted indecent behaviour or exhibitions.

There were the mysteriously named 'unnatural crimes' which our instructors failed to describe adequately, and a curious set of laws about indecent exposure of what is euphemistically called 'the person'. There were many legal discussions which tried to define precisely what our Victorian legislators meant when they made it illegal for a man indecently to expose his 'person'; we noted there was nothing in that Act which made it illegal for a woman indecently to expose *her* person, whatever that would have meant. Such were the privileges of our ladies. But we never did find out what a 'person' was, and the name 'flasher' was given to those pathetic fellows who performed this curious public display.

There were 'peepers' too, sometimes called 'pimpers'. These were seedy men of all ages who spied on ladies undressing, either on the beach or in their homes, hotels or boarding house bedrooms. It is amazing how many women insist on undressing before a lighted window without curtains, and this attracts many men with binoculars. They are attracted to the light as moths to a candle flame. This activity also brought complaints from the neighbours, which was how we became involved. As a result, we frequently offered 'suitable advice' to the ladies in question – we told them to close their curtains properly when undressing.

It is men of that propensity who hang around car-parks, beauty spots and picnic areas, there to observe the events of nature which occur when courting couples are engrossed in their overtures to one another. Because this behaviour terrifies ordinary folk, we had to patrol in an attempt to deter these nuisances.

Armed with this knowledge, therefore, the constabulary set about keeping order among the frisky holiday-makers. It is true to say that this aspect of our duty did keep us busy. We received many complaints about men indecently touching women on buses and in queues, of men using the pay-telescope on the clifftop to watch women struggling to undress decently behind deckchairs on the beach, of pimpers galore and flashers by the dozen.

It was with the purity of the town in mind that the Superintendent was alarmed to learn that a newly formed local Working Men's Club had hired a belly dancer as the finale for the entertainment scheduled for its opening night. He was rather worried about the town's image in case this turned out to be a stripper, but he was also worried that the police could be criticized if they failed to take any action to stem this flow of overt sensuality.

Because such clubs had rather tight membership rules, he and his advisers considered it was impossible to smuggle a local police officer into the club as an undercover agent to observe the proceedings. This meant that subterfuge was called for. As the club was a new one, the Superintendent decided that I and another young constable called Dave Carter would join the club, with the sole purpose of infiltrating that entertainment. We had to observe the proceedings in detail and report back to the Superintendent through our immediate superiors.

Both Dave and I were unknown to the committee, so we applied for membership, giving our lodgings as our addresses and stating we were employed by the Ministry of Agriculture as Contagious Diseases of Animals Inspectors. We were accepted without question and provided with membership cards. The Superintendent was delighted, and on the evening of the big event we dressed in civilian clothes and he took us aside to outline our final brief.

We were not to reveal our identities; we merely had to sit through the rumoured 'indecent performance' and take copious notes about the bodily actions, general behaviour and suggestive words or actions used by the belly dancer. We had not to arrest anyone or report anyone for summons – that possibility would be left for a decision by senior officers when they had carefully studied our report. We were there simply to report the facts. We said we knew what to do, and we were looking forward to this duty.

We were admitted without a second glance from the doorman and went to the bar, where we each purchased a pint of beer with our official expenses. Then, after half an hour, we were asked to take our seats in the big room for the evening's entertainment. We found a discreet table close to one of the exits, just in case we had to make a hurried departure. I noted that the audience comprised men and women.

There were speeches of welcome from officials, who outlined the club's future policies and who listed some forthcoming attractions later in the year. These included noted northern comedians, singers and entertainers. After the announcements, there followed a bawdy comedian who had us falling about with laughter. Very efficiently, he warmed up the audience. A male singer did a spot, then a trumpet player, who was followed by a group of singer-musicians with guitars. Finally, it was the turn of the belly dancer. She was top of the bill and had two spots;

the audience, suitably mellow after the earlier acts, eagerly awaited her turn.

Our moment had come, but we daren't take out our note-books. That would be too obvious – we decided to observe events and then jointly compile our report by relying upon our memories and powers of observation for the details.

A grand piano was pushed onto the side of the stage, and to resounding cheers the dancer's pianist emerged. He was a young man in evening dress, and he took his seat with elegance and style. A hush descended as he began to play. To my surprise, it was a piece of classical music, and everyone sat in a hushed silence, awaiting the delights which were to follow. There was a ripple in the curtains at the side of the stage, and as they parted, a tall, lithe young woman emerged. She was as thin as bean pole, and she was dancing divinely – but she was performing a sequence from the Nutcracker Suite.

There was a momentary buzz of curious anticipation from the audience, but they settled down and watched her. She was graceful and beautiful, and she completed her first spot with charm and undoubted skill. But everyone was waiting for her suddenly to switch into a dramatic and sensuous belly-dancing routine.

After her first spot, which comprised several well-known ballet routines, she went off to polite applause, following which there were some urgent movements behind the curtains. They parted and the club secretary hurried onto the stage. We felt he looked rather sheepish and embarrassed as he caught us before we dispersed for a five-minute break.

'Lads,' he said. 'There's been a mistake. Sorry about it. I rang t'agency in London to book a belly dancer, but they don't understand English down there. They've sent us this slip of a lass, she's a ballet dancer . . .'

'Bring t'lass back on!' shouted somebody from the audience. 'She's worth watching.'

And this was followed spontaneously by a loud cheer. So after we'd replenished our glasses, she came back to complete a dazzling ballet routine. She was cheered to an encore and won more affection from that audience than any of the other turns.

She was given a right good Yorkshire welcome, and I was proud of my fellow club members. She would remember her visit to Strensford, just as I would remember my first spell of covert police work.

Flashers are probably the most harmless and ineffective of men and yet, by their peculiar behaviour, they are regarded as ogres, sexual maniacs or dangerous, evil monsters. These unfortunates are likely to be sexually inadequate so far as mature women are concerned and would probably flee home to the safety of mother if a woman responded to their weird form of romantic advance.

To go about their performance, they frequently conform to their cartoon image by dressing in dirty, loose-fitting raincoats and little else, for this device enables them to fling open the raincoat at an opportune moment and so compel some embarrassed women or girl to view their impressive, naked pride and joy, i.e. the male appendage known to the Victorian legislators as 'the person'.

It is not the task of the police to understand why they behave in this curious manner. Their job is to deal with them in accordance with the rule of law, and there are three provisions by which this can be effected, all of which operate on the basis that such behaviour constitutes a nuisance.

The first of those provisions is Common Law. This is the ancient code of practice from which most of our legislation has descended, and this decided centuries ago that exposure of the naked person was a public nuisance. This means that men or women may be guilty of an offence if the incident occurs in public, but few men ever complained if they noticed a naked woman in a public place.

Then in 1824, a few years before Victoria came to the throne, our legislators produced their famous Vagrancy Act. This made it an offence for a man 'wilfully, openly, lewdly and obscenely to expose his person with intent to insult a female', and this offence could occur either in private or in public. However, it was necessary to show that the flasher intended to insult a female. 'Insult' is the word, not 'impress', and it was this Act which appears to infer that only men may be guilty of exposing 'the person'.

A few years later, in 1847, the Town Police Clauses Act, which was, and perhaps still is, in force only in certain urban areas, created another form of this offence. It said that it was unlawful 'wilfully and indecently to expose the person in any street in any urban district where the act is in force, to the annoyance of residents or passengers'.

We had to learn the subtle differences between all three provisions. The Vagrancy Act appears to apply only to men, while Common Law and the Town Police Clauses Act do seem to cater for female flashers who misbehave in public, although the Town Police Clauses Act does specify that someone must be annoyed. The three variations of this offence do differ in various ways.

Suppose a female flasher operates in private, or on the top deck of a bus, or on a pleasure steamer? Or suppose that, even though she did flash in public, no one complained that they were annoyed? Is the law then broken or not?

In an attempt to understand these statutes, we would dream up situations which were designed to test the precise meaning of these three provisions, because every word is important. For an offence to be committed, every word counts. And then, in the present century, we encountered streakers, naked people of either sex who dashed through busy places for a laugh. Did they offend against any of these provisions? Was anyone insulted or annoyed, or was it just a laugh? The law is so precise in the use of its words that policemen must think carefully before they act or make an arrest.

If the academic side of these three laws exercised our minds and gave us lots of laughs, the practical aspects also provided a good deal of amusement during that summer in Strensford.

The first occasion came from a middle-age spinster living in a flat on the West Cliff. Her complaint was that a neighbour, a man in his late twenties, regularly indecently exposed himself to her, and so I was despatched to interview her about it. I listened to her tale of woe and asked her to show me from where the man operated. She took me to her bedroom and made me stand on a chair so that I could look into his bedroom . . .

We took no action in that case, except to tell the fellow that he was the centre of some attention from a lady pimper who had to stand on a chair in order to view him in his naked splendour.

The other occasion was more serious and baffling because we came to appreciate that we had a cunning and persistent flasher on our patch. Even though he never physically touched his victims, he fitted the traditional image because he did wear an old raincoat and he did confront lone women on the streets, whereupon he would fling open his raincoat to display his impressive wares.

He operated both in daylight and in the darkness, and his behaviour became very frightening for two reasons – first, he wore a woollen balaclava mask over his face, and secondly, he always operated in thick fog. After making his victim scream with shock, he would vanish, leaving her with the terrifying task of making her solitary way home in that same, dense, clinging fog.

In all cases, he used the streets, and in all cases the state of his rampant 'person' provided ample evidence of his intention to insult a female. This meant that, when we caught him, he would be proceeded against under the provisions of the Vagrancy Act 1824. This gave the police the power to arrest him, and the magistrates' court the power to declare him a Rogue and Vagabond!

The link with the fog rapidly dawned upon us because whenever there descended one of those dense coastal sea frets, known locally as roaks, he would emerge. Dawn, noon or night made no difference, but he did seem to know precisely where to locate women who were either working alone or walking alone in the town. Examples included a cinema usherette walking home after work, two girls from a small factory walking home at lunchtime, a shop assistant locking up her premises, a visitor walking down the pier, a fish-and-chip-shop lady tidying up after closing time . . .

In all cases, it had been foggy, and the fog horn had been wailing in the dense white blanket which suppressed most of the other sounds. We did wonder if the sombre blasting of the fog horn affected his horn in this odd way, but his activities reached a stage where something positive had to be done, and done efficiently. We had to hunt him down, rather than wait until we discovered him in action.

But in a large area of a town, with all its streets, shops, houses, factories and other premises, and with twenty-four hours at one's disposal, how could we begin to trace him? Other than the fog links, there were no indications that he operated to a system. It seemed he simply roamed in the fog and selected his victims at random.

We missed him three times. One night we were positioned at several strategic locations in town, places where women would be alone. I was concealed near a local pub whose barmaid cycled home alone at closing time, but he did not strike that night. Instead he went into the suburbs and flashed himself at a woman walking her dog in the fog.

In spite of the nature of his operations, we never publicized them in the Press; if we had, we might have stopped him for a time, but we would never have caught him. That discreet silence probably meant he was unaware of our growing dossier on him, and it would, we hoped, encourage him to be careless. We were sure that one day he would make an error.

Another aspect of this patience was that, by our silence, we did not unduly terrify the ladies of the town. It was true that the victims did talk about it to their friends, and that some very localized rumours did spread – rumours that suggested a sexual maniac was lurking in every shadowy side street with intent to ravish every female in the town – but the lack of general publicity was to our advantage, and it prevented widespread alarm in the town.

But due to the growing list of complaints, the Superintendent decided that a decoy must be used. A policeman was clearly of no value because our flasher would never operate if there was a man in the vicinity, so the Superintendent sought the co-operation of Scarborough Police. The Superintendent at Scarborough agreed his policewoman should help.

The outcome was that, whenever a sea fog descended upon Strensford, we had to ring Scarborough Police and they would immediately send an available policewoman to Strensford, a matter of thirty minutes' drive. She would patrol in plain clothes in an attempt to tempt and then trap 'The Strensford Flasher'. It was all we could do – there was no resident policewoman at Strensford, and we felt it was not a job we dared entrust to the keenest of civilian volunteers, however well backed up she might be with our own reinforcements.

The problem was that the Scarborough policewoman was with us only for about six hours out of the twenty-four and only on the days when she could come to Strensford. It was a forlorn hope that she would ever be in the right place at the right time. The chances of a policewoman being his victim were remote to say the least. There were tens of thousands of vulnerable women in the town.

Sure enough, at eleven o'clock one night, an hour after she had left to return to her own station, he flashed at a waitress as she was leaving a restaurant. On another occasion, our police-woman was patrolling the area near the laundry. She had been told to patrol there, in civilian clothes and in the fog, because the laundry workers were due to depart at the end of their shift. He had never been reported in action at that location, and it was thought highly likely that sooner or later he would turn up there. But he didn't, at least not on that occasion. He performed outside a fancy-goods shop whose manageress was quick enough to throw a cheap plaster ornament at him. But she missed. The ornament smashed on the pavement, and he vanished into the all-embracing mist.

We could not give up now. Sooner or later someone from the town council or from the Townswomen's Guild or some other formal organization would be making an official complaint about our lack of success. The resultant publicity would frighten him into lying low for a long time, and he'd emerge later to continue a new series of flashings. While it was true that a halt to his activities could be beneficial in the short term, we needed to catch him and arraign him before the magistrates because of all his stupidity and the terror he was creating. And we were still confident he did not know that we were aware of all his previous behaviour.

Then one summer afternoon, soon after lunch, a thick fog descended. It completely enveloped the town for it was a chilling sea roak of very dense proportions. It saturated everything with its droplets of clinging cold moisture. People came in from the beach, and others evacuated the town centre to go to their hotels, boarding houses or homes. Some sought shelter in the shops and amusement arcades, while the cafés did a roaring trade in hot drinks.

As the people moved about the place, their heads were covered with the droplets, their clothes were saturated and their flesh was chilled to the proverbial bone. It was a thorough pea-souper of a fog, a fog to end all fogs, and the fog horn high on the cliff was bellowing its sombre warning to ships off shore.

But this weather was ideal for the Strensford Flasher; it was his kind of afternoon, if a little cold for long exposures, and so we urgently requested a policewoman from Scarborough. She came by train because of the fog-bound condition of the coastal road, and she arrived just before four o'clock.

This was Monica Wilson, a nice-looking and very capable girl of about twenty-eight. In her civilian clothes she was highly attractive and she knew the town fairly well as she had been with us on some previous Flashing assignments.

I was on duty that afternoon, and during a small conference in the muster room we discussed the Flasher's previous venues and the action we would take if Monica called for assistance. For urgent communication we had to rely on shouts or whistles; Monica was capable of fully utilizing both.

One thing of some importance did emerge from that conference. We learned that the Flasher had never used a venue more than once. He had zoomed in, flashed and left, never to return to the same place. This helped a great deal because it meant we could eliminate a lot of possible venues.

Monica listened and made notes, and then suggested she patrol near the railway station. Her logic was that many office workers would be making their way to the station for the 5.35 p.m. train to Middlesbrough, and so would many miserable holiday-makers whose day out had been curtailed by the chilling fog. It seemed a good idea, and everyone agreed.

She was backed by six uniformed constables, one plain-clothes detective, two sergeants and the Inspector, and we all had had our orders in the event of a call from Monica.

We had a feeling he would arrive; there was that tingling air of expectancy as we vanished into yards, alleys, shops; we lurked behind the portals of the railway station and the bus station, and we realized that today we did have a possible timetable for what we hoped would be his last great flash.

We were all in position by five o'clock. The train left at 5.35 p.m. and so provided Monica with a period of thirty-five minutes in which to make a name for herself by capturing the Strensford Flasher.

It was an eerie sensation, waiting in the silence of that great cold roak, with visibility only a very few feet, but this time we were successful. Or rather, Monica was.

We heard her shout; we rushed to her aid, and there in the fog she had arrested the Flasher. Of all the people he could have selected, he had flashed before Monica, who, unimpressed by his credentials, had rushed at him and now had him in a strong, firm grip. She was proudly marching him towards the police station.

With her free hand, she had removed his balaclava, but I did not recognize him, and so, before a growing crowd of well-wishers and sightseers, she towed him toward the police station.

But it was her mode of seizure which impressed everyone, because Monica, thinking fast and acting as quickly, had seized him by that collection of male equipment the Victorians had christened 'the person'.

He had tears in his eyes as we allowed her to steer him to his just rewards. The Strensford Flasher had flashed his last.

Another recurring problem of a similar type was that of pimpers, those who peep secretly at courting couples or peer through gaping curtains at night, hoping to catch a glimpse of bare flesh or ladies' underwear.

One such man received swift punishment when he was peering into a ground-floor flat. He was intent on watching a woman undress for bed and became so excited at what he saw that he wished to share his experience with passers-by. He broke cover and beckoned a man who was walking his dog along the adjacent street, and the man, who showed some interest in this event, padded across the lawn to have a look. Having looked and understood, he promptly felled the pimper with one swift blow of a very powerful fist. The pimper had been observing that man's rather luscious wife.

Because there was no law which expressly forbade this obnoxious conduct, the police (if they caught a pimper) had to rely on the six-hundred-year-old Justice of the Peace Act of 1361 (34 Edw. III cl. 1360–1). This gave the magistrates a wonderfully flexible power to bind over those who were guilty of conduct which was likely to cause a breach of the peace. Many would argue that peeping through curtained windows at night was conduct which was very likely to cause a breach of the peace, as was illustrated by the judicial flattening of the pimper I've mentioned above. And so, if and when we caught anyone behaving in this way, we took him to court, where we presented all the salacious facts for the benefit of the magistrates, the Press and ultimately the public. And we smiled as the court publicly bound over the pimper to be of good behaviour. This usually did the trick, the resultant publicity being more than an adequate deterrent to others.

We all reckoned Edward III was a very wise man when he made this highly flexible preventative law. It is still widely used to bind over silly people to be of good behaviour, or to keep the peace, sometimes with a penalty if they fail or refuse to abide by the court's ruling.

In many ways, 34 Edw. III cl. 1360–1 was tailor-made for dealing with pimpers, but there was one little snag – we had to catch the pimpers in the act.

The one place which gave us more problems than any other, because of its compulsive attraction to pimpers, was the Nurses' Home. Situated just behind the police station, it was a new brick-built construction designed to be the home of forty-eight single nurses who worked at Strensford Memorial Hospital. But the truth was that only a dozen or so required this kind of accommodation, and so the home was greatly under-used.

Owing to their long shifts, only some six or eight nurses were present in the building at any one time, and the authorities had closed off the top two storeys.

It was argued that eventually, when the hospital expanded to its full potential, the whole of the building would be utilized, but when I was at Strensford, there was no likelihood of this. So the upper floors were closed, and left undecorated, unheated and far from welcoming. This meant that the small band of resident nurses used the ground floor, which boasted such facilities as the kitchen, lounge, laundry and other offices.

Because they slept at ground level, and because women are notoriously poor at properly closing their bedroom curtains, the narrow slits of light which emanated therefrom, were just too much for the town's army of pimpers. Like moths being drawn to a flame, they crossed the lawns and pushed through shrubs in the hope they would see something more thrilling than last time. Quite often they did catch glimpses of female flesh which thrilled them, and the word got around. At any one time, several pimpers might be concealed in the shrubbery, all breathing heavily as the nurses went about their personal and private tasks.

The police station, therefore, received regular panic calls from the matron, as a result of which patrols were organized from time to time. The girls were advised how to close their curtains and why to close their curtains, and for a short time afterwards the pimpers turned their attentions elsewhere. But, within a week or so, they were back because some curtains had been left an inch or so open, so the whole circus started anew.

We never did catch a pimper at the Nurses' Home, for the simple reason that its hilltop site meant that the lurking lechers could observe the approach of any constable well in advance of his arrival, and so vanish until another time. This being so, there was always the possibility that a nurse would peer out just in time to observe the timely arrival of a policeman, and so come to believe that the town's constables were pimping. Such are the risks of police duty.

But we did have the last laugh.

During one weekend that summer, the whole of the county

constabulary was ordered to take part in a joint military and police exercise. It was called Exercise Viking, the idea that army volunteers would attempt to enter several unspecified police stations throughout the county. It was being done so that the security procedures at all police stations would be thoroughly tested. Forty-five soldiers were to act as infiltrators and they were to begin their subversive mission at 6 a.m. one Sunday. For reasons which we failed to understand, they were to operate from a base at Strensford, a factor which meant that our police station was not a target.

The CO came to the Superintendent to ask if there was any premises which would provide primitive accommodation for his men during that Saturday night. A church hall would be ideal, as they'd bring sleeping-bags. But the Superintendent, being a man of imagination, had a brainwave which was due somewhat to another call from the matron of the Memorial Hospital. She had a further complaint about pimpers.

'Matron,' he oozed, 'I know that beneath that starched front of yours, there is a heart of gold. Now, I need help – can you accommodate forty-five young men next Saturday night? I need beds for them between about 11 p.m. and 6 a.m. They'll be out by six next morning at the latest. They're soldiers, and they'll bring sleeping-bags.'

'Soldiers? In the hospital? You must be joking! They're not ill, are they?'

'I wasn't thinking of the hospital, matron. I was thinking of your Nurses' Home, all that empty space. That would be ideal. Haven't you a large number of empty beds?'

'But I can't mix soldiers with my nurses, in the same building!'

'I thought each floor was self-contained,' he continued.

'Well, up to a point, but there are common areas, such as the lounge, kitchen and so on, and there are internal linking staircases.'

'I thought these men might help us catch those pimpers,' he added shrewdly. 'I can imagine a pimper finding a soldier there instead of a nurse . . .'

'You could make use of the room, I'm sure, Superintendent,

if they were not being used by my girls. With the consent of the hospital authorities, of course, but . . .'

'I've accommodation for ten people in the police station, matron. We've good, warm, cosy beds. They used to be the single men's quarters, so they're very well appointed. We keep them in case of emergencies . . . ten men could sleep here, and thirty-five could come to your spacious home and use the upper floors.'

'I cannot have mixed sexes under one roof, Superintendent. That is final. But I have had a thought. I might persuade those girls who are here on that Saturday to come down to the police station, under supervision, of course . . .'

'I would arrange for a woman police officer to be on duty,' he said, craftily smiling to himself.

'And if I had an emergency at the hospital, your men would run any nurse to the wards, to be in attendance just as if she had been in the Home?'

'Of course,' he beamed. 'And then all the soldiers could make use of your premises, just for one night. There is no question of feeding them, or supplying bed linen. They just need a bed to support their sleeping-bags, nothing more.'

'I'll have to put it to the nurses in question,' she said.

They thought it was a marvellous idea. The prospect of all those men so near was a thrill too, so the nurses, only eight of them, agreed to use the single men's quarters at the police station for just one night while their own beds, on all floors, were utilized by the soldiers.

The officer in charge, a young captain, was asked to visit the Superintendent, who sought assurance that there would be decorum from all ranks. The matron must not be upset.

'Oh, and Captain,' said the Superintendent. 'There is one other matter. Over the recent months we have had bother from pimpers around that Nurses' Home. Ask your fellows to close their curtains, eh? Especially those on the ground floor? We don't want pimpers spying upon a lot hairy soldiers, do we?'

'I'll acquaint them, sir,' said the Captain.

He did, and some promptly left their curtains open and kept

watch, hoping to teach the said pimper(s) a lesson. It should provide an evening's sport.

It was midnight when there was a scuffle in the entrance to the police station, and I was on night duty. I left the security of the office and saw two soldiers dragging a youth into the interior. He was crying, and they were dressed in pyjama tops with army uniform trousers.

'We've got your pimper, mate,' said one, throwing the hapless youth to the floor. 'The lads got him, mind, and gave him what-for.'

'What was he doing?' I asked as I gripped the collar of the youth and dragged him to his feet. He was small and limp and weeping softly.

'Pimping through the curtains,' said one of them. 'A few minutes ago, as the lads were undressing.'

'Right,' I said to the youth. 'Get in there. So you're the one who's been bothering those nurses, eh?'

'No, sir,' he simpered, his wrists hanging limp and his body wriggling like a worm. 'I haven't been to see the nurses. I just like looking at soldiers . . .'

9

Our deeds still travel with us from afar,
And what we have been makes us what we are.

George Eliot, 1819–80

When I was patrolling the sea front at Strensford, there were
times when I wondered how the holiday-makers acquired the
amount of money they spent so freely. Young people, some with
tiny children, appeared to have limitless amounts of cash which
they spent on their endless fun.

My police income was so small that it allowed me to feed and
clothe my growing family, who were at home while I enjoyed
this spell of seaside duty, but there was nothing left for holidays
or luxuries. I knew it was wrong to be envious of others because,
after all, I had chosen this career and had known the salary
structure before I joined. If I wanted their kind of riches and a
life of holidays and fun, the remedy was in my own hands. I
would have to leave the Force and do something else. But what
could I do? Besides, what other job offered such a variety of
work, with such a lot of contact with the public and so many
interesting and varied occurrences?

Nonetheless, I must admit that I did wonder what other
people did for a living; I wondered how they could afford so
much time off with so much spending money.

Those musings reached their pinnacle one Saturday night as I
patrolled Strensford's West Cliff area. It was here that the best
hotels could be found, and in the summer months they were
always busy. One or two of them organized Saturday-night

dances, or even dinner-dances, and whilst these were chiefly for the benefit of guests and their friends, some were open to the public – at a cost. It was the high price which kept at bay the riff-raff who frequented other Saturday-night hops and who caused trouble of various kinds.

There were few major problems at those hotel dances although we did patrol the streets outside, partly as a deterrent to passing or possible trouble-makers, and partly to ensure that visiting cars were correctly parked and lit. A small number of streets remained illuminated throughout the night but an unlit parked car on a dark street could be a hazard.

Such cars provided one of our minor worries. In those days, all cars which were parked on the streets overnight were supposed to leave their sidelights burning, and although the police did occasionally turn a blind eye to some, such as those in cul-de-sacs or quiet side streets, we did insist that those on the main roads, thoroughfares and busy streets should conform to the law, if only for reasons of safety. Many visitors were caught out by this because in some larger towns the local councils had made byelaws which allowed overnight street parking without lights in designated areas. Visitors from those areas wrongly believed that their system applied throughout the country, and they got a ticket.

But we seldom took the offenders to court. We put a ticket on the offending car, and eventually the owner received a 'caution' – a warning letter from the Superintendent stressing that he must not in that way offend again.

One surprising aspect of these vehicles was that many visitors left their car doors unlocked all night, and it is fair to say that thieving was not the problem it is today. It was very seldom we received a report of a theft from an unlocked car, but this act of trust (or carelessness) did enable us to switch on the lights of many cars which were left parked on the main roads. That small act was our good turn for the driver, even if it did flatten the battery.

One Saturday night, somewhere around 11.15 p.m., I was making my slow way around my beat. I was moving along a wide main street which boasted several hotels, and the largest, the

King's Head, was having one of its dances. A row of expensive cars was parked outside.

I noticed that the one at the front was not displaying any lights, and so I approached it to see if the driver was still there. He wasn't, but I strolled around to examine and admire it. It was a gleaming Jaguar in dark blue. Because of its colour, it would be difficult to see by an approaching motorist, and for safety's sake it needed lights. I tried the driver's door, and it was unlocked. I reached inside, and as I did so, the strong scent of leather upholstery and rich carpets met me. The car reeked of quality. After a few moments searching, I found the light switch. I switched on the sidelights, but while my head was inside the vehicle and the interior lights were on, I took the opportunity to admire the interior – the intricate dashboard, the walnut fascia, the dials, the plush seats, the position of the interior lights . . .

It was then that I noticed a briefcase. It was lying on the back seat and was like a small, black suitcase; furthermore, it was open, and astonishingly it was full of money. There were notes galore, £5 notes and £1 notes. I had never seen so much cash, not even on a bank counter.

This placed me in an immediate dilemma. If I left it as it was, so easily visible from the pavement, someone might steal it. I could not secure the car – there weren't internal locks on all doors as there are in modern vehicles. I could, I suppose, close the case lid to conceal its contents, and then push it out of sight under one of the seats. Or I could take the case down to the police station for safe custody.

In those days, without personal radio sets or the help of the Police National Computer, immediate assistance and advice were not available. For one thing, I could not trace the name of the owner of the car. That would have to wait until the Local Registration Office opened on Monday morning.

The boot was locked, so I closed the lid of the briefcase and removed it to the driver's seat, where I placed it on the floor, partly under the seat. It would not fit completely beneath, so I placed a rubber floor-mat on top of it, hoping at least it would be safe from prying eyes and therefore less open to temptation. I could lock the rear doors by depressing the internal handles and likewise the front passenger's door. But I had to leave the driver's door unlocked, for without a key I could not secure it.

I now decided to search for the driver. He was surely at the dance in the King's Head, so, having made a note of the car number, I went in. At the reception desk, I checked to see if the owner was a resident, for the hotel register contained the residents' car numbers, but it was not there. I asked the receptionist if she would use the tannoy system to ask the driver to come to the front foyer, where I would meet him. I explained it was an urgent matter.

I heard the Jaguar's registration number being relayed throughout the hotel and its dance floor, but after five minutes and two repeats of my message, no one appeared. I thanked the girl and requested that if the driver did come to her desk, she ask him to check his car thoroughly. I thought a vague sort of message would not draw too much unwelcome attention to it.

An hour later, I met Sergeant White, our supervisory officer for that shift, and told him of my discovery and my actions.

'Oh, bloody hell! Is he in town?'

'You know him?'

'Know him? Everybody knows him. Wasn't he at that dance?'

'If he was, he never emerged when I called him. Who is this man, sarge?'

'Leo Farrand. A real character, once seen, never forgotten. Forget about the money – he's so bloody careless, he wouldn't know, or even care, if it did get nicked.'

'You're joking!' I cried. 'There must have been thousands of pounds in that case.'

'He always carries about five thousand around with him, in cash. And when he gets drunk, he gives it all away. Seriously! I'm not joking.'

I learned from Sergeant White that Leo Farrand lived, at least some of the time, at Keldholme Hall, which lay in a fold in the valley about five miles out of Strensford. When he was not in residence there, he lived in London, and the sergeant said that Farrand's antics had caused the local police to believe he was involved in big-time crime in London, or that his money was forged. Accordingly, they had contacted Scotland Yard for discreet enquiries to be made into his background, but he was no criminal, nor was he ever suspected by them of being one. In fact, he was a Harley Street specialist, a very clever man whose specialization was dental matters.

'Because of our suspicions,' continued Sergeant White as we patrolled the streets, 'we got hold of some of his notes, but they were genuine. It seems he is honest, if somewhat stupid. Now, whether he comes up north just to get away from the pressures of the city, we don't know, but when he does come, he certainly makes his presence felt. He does so by getting drunk and throwing money away. He throws it about like confetti. Literally, I mean.'

I asked the sergeant to describe him so that I would know him, and he told me that Farrand was very tall, probably about six feet two or three inches, and on the thin side. He had a mop of thick black hair and wore a black moustache and a small black, neatly trimmed goatee beard. He was about forty-five years old, and he always dressed in a flamboyant fashion, often wearing a black cloak with a purple silk lining. I could imagine this character dressed in a top hat and tails, being a magician on stage or an actor in a Gothic drama of some kind. I could visualize him in a horror film or acting as a handsome lover in manorial surroundings. He sounded fascinating, and so I thereupon decided to do my best to catch sight of him.

But I did not see him that Saturday night. My beat took me away from the vicinity of the King's Head, and when I returned in the early hours, the car had gone. There was no report of his cash being stolen, so I guessed he'd gone quietly home.

Within two weeks I did see him. I was despatched upon a spell of duty at Glenesk Mart, a busy cattlemarket two miles into the valley of Strensbeck. Because the local constable was sick, I had to deputize for him by issuing licences at the market.

I positioned myself in the little wooden hut for the afternoon and set about issuing dozens of licences which authorized pigs to be removed from the mart to various destinations. This was really a form of record in case swine fever or foot-and-mouth disease broke out. Through these licences, the police or the Ministry of Agriculture could trace the movements of any suspect animal. It wasn't a difficult job, but some market traders and attenders were merry because the pubs were open all day. This was known as a General Order of Exemption, and it locally extended normal licensing hours so that the pubs were open all day for the refreshment of those who were attending the market.

It seemed that Leo Farrand had decided to attend that market and that he had also availed himself of the abundance of liquor. I learned of this when there was a good deal of shouting at a disturbance near the pub, so I had to temporarily abandon my pig licences to find out what was happening.

From Sergeant White's description, and the actions of the central character of that fracas, it was easy to recognize Leo. I walked to the scene of the bother – we always walked slowly to any centre of bother, the reason being that we had time to determine our course of action before arrival. It also allowed some of the aggravation to evaporate before it was our turn to join in. This simple strategy invariably paid dividends. By the time we arrived, the protagonists had knocked themselves silly, and we simply swept up the pieces.

As I approached, I could see Leo's tall, dramatic figure. He was violently waving his arms as he showered money around the front door of the pub. Even as I approached, the air was full of paper money which fluttered to earth as a crowd gathered around him.

To my surprise, none of the crowd seemed to be keeping the money. As Leo delved into his briefcase and hurled untold numbers of notes into the sky, the crowd were rushing around and collecting them, then stuffing them back into his case. And he simply threw them sky-high again. He was laughing as he did so, and it seemed more like a very expensive game than something which could develop into a fight.

I began to wonder if this could be considered 'conduct likely to cause a breach of the peace', for among greedy people such behaviour could certainly intensify into a mad scramble for the cash, with fists and feet flying as everyone tried to acquire Leo's free riches. But I could imagine the comments in court and in the Press, if I arrested a man for throwing away his own money.

Leo saw me as I approached.

'Why, hello,' he boomed, his loud, strong voice matching his personality. 'It's the law. Now, constable, are you coming to join the scramble for gold?'

'No,' I said. 'And I think you'd better stop too.'

The crowd began to grumble – I was spoiling their fun, so I had to think fast.

'These notes are all fakes,' I shouted at the crowd. 'We've been after this chap for a long time. Anyone caught with a fake note in his possession could be sent to prison. So, come on, put them all back and let's settle down.'

My subterfuge worked. Several people threw notes onto the ground, and Leo and I spent time packing them into his case.

'They're not fakes, constable,' he said with a slight slur to his words as we rammed the notes into the case. 'It's real money, every single note of it.'

'I know, but you can't go throwing your money about like that!' I said. 'It's just not done.'

'Why not?' he stood to his full, majestic height. 'Why can I not throw money away? It is mine. I can do as I please with it, surely?'

He could, of course. There was no law to prevent him, and yet, somehow, this did not make me happy. Perhaps it was because policemen earn their cash by such a long, hard and thankless struggle that there seemed to be something morally wrong, rather than legally wrong, in doing as he was.

'You were obstructing the footpath,' I said, thinking fast. 'And I think you've had too much to drink. Where's your car?'

'I came by train,' he said. 'It's market day, and I knew I'd be getting too much liquor, so I came by train. I won't drive my car home when I'm drunk, constable. That *would* be asking for trouble, wouldn't it?'

'So what will you do now?'

He was fastening the lid of his briefcase. 'I will make my way home,' he said. 'And I will have some tea, and then tonight I might go out for a meal.'

'With all this money?'

'I might find someone who welcomes my generosity,' he said. 'Those farmers were handing it all back.'

'They're honest men, Mr Farrand. They deal in cash all day

and every day, and they know the value of money. They'll score points over each other quite happily in a deal, but they won't *steal* another's cash. You were lucky it was them, and not a crowd of villains. They were just enjoying the game.'

'But I wanted them to have my money,' he said. 'Why don't people want my money?'

'Dunno,' I said. 'But look, if you want to give it away, why not send it to a charity, something like Red Cross or the lifeboats or the church, somewhere it will do a lot of good?'

'I do,' his voice was definitely slurred. 'And when I've a lot left over, I give more away. Now, what's wrong in that, constable? Tell me why I cannot give away my own money.'

There was no reason, of course. I could not think of anything logical to say, so I merely shrugged my shoulders then added.

'Well, when you do give it away, don't let it hurt people, eh? Don't let it cause fights and greed or trouble of any kind, Mr Farrand.'

'If you say so, constable,' and he wandered off, heading for the railway station with his case of notes clutched in his hand.

Later I heard he'd been to a village pub high in Strensbeck Valley where he'd given away hundreds of pounds to everyone in the place, and had bought drinks all night. On another occasion he'd gone to an agricultural show in the valley and done the same.

I saw him once more before my tour of duty was over. Dressed in his flowing cape and with a Robin Hood type of hat on his head, he was standing at the west end of the bridge which split the town as it spanned the harbour. He had what appeared to be a cinema usherette's tray held before his tall figure by a cord slung around his neck, and he was offering pound notes to everyone who crossed the bridge.

But no one took his money.

He noticed my interest and beckoned to me. I strolled across and greeted him.

'Hello, again, Mr Farrand. How's business?'

'Would you believe no one wants my money?' he said. 'I've heard about this sort of thing happening – I did it on Westminster Bridge, you know, right in the heart of London, and no one would accept my money. Now the same's happening here in

Yorkshire. I find life is very odd.'

'It is very odd,' I agreed. 'You just can't understand people.'

Another fascinating Strensford character was a policeman, a grizzled old constable who was almost at the end of his service. I saw little of him because his shifts and mine seldom corresponded, but like many officers in the North Riding I had heard of his exploits, and his name was something of a byword in local police folklore.

He was Max Cooper, a heavily built and very jovial character who had seen his fortieth birthday some years ago. He was what we termed an old-stager, a man totally satisfied with life. He was totally content with his lot and had never even attempted his exams; for Max, promotion was regarded as greasing up to one's superiors.

He had the chubby, pink face of a countryman with a strikingly clear complexion, although his hair had thinned almost to the point of extinction. His hobbies were fishing, which absorbed him almost totally, and drinking, which he undertook with gusto. Overall, Max had an infectiously carefree attitude to work and to life in general. In other words, he did as he liked, and he was one of those men with whom 'nowt could be done'.

No one, not even the sternest superintendent, could dictate to this stolid Yorkshireman. It was possible to persuade him to adopt a certain path but never to drive him. When he executed his night-shifts, for example, he took with him some extra comforts, which included a small alarm clock, an inflatable rubber cushion and a flask of coffee. The rest of us left our flasks at the station, but Max didn't. He carried his around his beat and claimed it kept him awake as he patrolled throughout the night hours.

Max's propensity was to fall asleep in strange places, and I did learn that, over the years, the locals had come to know him and his odd trait. Most of them therefore refrained from calling out the ambulance or the police when they found a hefty policeman apparently dead or drunk or possibly asleep in their greenhouse or coalshed.

Strensford's seasonal visitors were not to know this, of course, and so it was not uncommon to receive reports of dead policemen in fishing cobles, touring buses, back alleys and telephone kiosks. In all cases, the 'corpse' was Max. It was this incurable habit which compelled him to carry the alarm clock and the cushion.

When making a point at a telephone kiosk, Max would go inside, inflate his cushion, place it on the floor and sit on it. As he waited in that comfortable position, he would set the alarm clock to rouse him just in time to walk to his next point, timed for half an hour later. Unfortunately, he regularly forgot to set his alarm, which meant he forgot to wake up as he sat curled up in his telephone kiosks. His absence from sundry appointed places meant that a search was made by his colleagues, just in case he had been assaulted or attacked or had even died.

It followed that Max was a problem to his supervisory officers, but somehow he avoided disciplinary charges for sleeping on, or for being absent from, his place of duty. Most of the time his colleagues covered up for him, for in the daylight hours he was a fine fellow, a very good policeman and a jolly asset to the town.

Now that I've left Strensford, two memories of him stand out in my mind.

One bright July morning, I paraded for duty at 5.50 a.m., in readiness for my early turn shift which ran from 6 a.m. until 2 p.m. We always reported ten minutes before the official start of any shift so we could be briefed about our forthcoming duties. By six, therefore, we were all ready to patrol the town, when the outgoing shift sergeant, a thin fellow with poor teeth, came into the Muster Room. He spoke to our sergeant, Sergeant White.

'Chalky,' he said so we could all hear. 'Max has done it again. He hasn't come in to book off duty. He'll be asleep somewhere. I'm sending two of my lads around all the likely places on his beat, but I thought your lot might keep their eyes open as well. I'll skin the bloody man alive, so I will. Why can't he come home to sleep like the rest of us, instead of kipping in kiosks and keeping us all out of bed?'

With no personal radio sets, we had to maintain contact with the police station through the network of telephone kiosk about the town and were told to ring in the moment we found him.

Then the search would be called off. But no one found him. I patrolled my town centre patch and checked pub toilets, cottage outhouses, garages, waste land, telephone kiosks, shop doorways, buses, cars – everything and everywhere that might have provided a bed for the slumbering Max.

The office duty constable rang us all to keep us informed of the nil result, and I rang the office in my turn to report a nil response. This lack of a result began to generate some concern. Even though we had searched all Max's regular nodding-off places, no one had found him – and he wasn't easily overlooked.

By 8.30 that same morning, there was increasing concern which amounted almost to panic. Because no one had found Max, it was genuinely feared that he had come to some harm – perhaps he'd fallen into the harbour, or been attacked by villains, or become ill and collapsed somewhere. So at 8.45 we were all summoned back to the station for a briefing. There we were told that a full-scale search would be mounted, with police dogs and more men being drafted in.

A last-minute check was made at his home, just in case he had wandered back, but he was not there. His wife, a big lady called Polly, was not in the least worried – she said he often went on fishing trips and didn't come home on time, because he had fallen asleep on a river bank somewhere. She was virtually unflappable – she knew him so well!

But the Force, in its official capacity, was worried, hence the preparations for a major search. The Inspector and the Superintendent had been called from their beds at the god-forsaken hour of 7.30 a.m., and we all assembled for this vital briefing.

The clock was striking nine as the Superintendent walked in to allocate to each one of us an area for intense search and thorough enquiry.

'You all know PC Cooper,' he said. 'Even those who are with us for temporary coastal duties are familiar with his appearance, so I need not bother with a physical description. Now, last night, he was patrolling No. 3 Beat . . .'

At that stage the constable on office duty gingerly opened the door of the Muster Room and poked his head around the corner.

'Sorry to interrupt, sir, but it is important. It's Max . . . er . . .

PC Cooper, sir. He's all right, he's on his way home sir . . . I just got a call . . .'

There was a long silence followed by murmurings of relief as the Superintendent, valiantly suppressing his anger, vanished upon his mission of discovery of the truth, while those who had remained on duty since six were dismissed and sent home for their overdue rest. I and the other early-turn men all returned to our normal duties, not daring at that stage, or in that tense official atmosphere, to attempt to discover what Max had done. We'd find out in due course.

Later that day I did find out where he had been.

We learned about 3 a.m. he had gone into the deserted railway station, as indeed we all did, and had entered a carriage for a sit-down. He had fallen asleep in a corner without setting his faithful alarm clock, and at 5.30 the empty coaches had been taken up the line to Middlesbrough. The sleeping Max had gone with them.

Strensford Station in those days closed after the last train at night, which was 5.35 p.m., and opened next morning around 6.45 a.m. The 7 a.m. train steamed up the valley to Middlesbrough and returned with a load of passengers, but on this occasion the empty coaches which had been left overnight in Strensford were required for an additional summer train from Middlesbrough. When they had arrived, they had been shunted into a siding, and so had Max. He had woken at 8.30 and, thinking the sun was higher than normal for the time of day, had emerged to find he was not in Strensford but in Middlesbrough, some thirty miles away. We were assured that this surprised him somewhat.

He was fined three days' pay for that lapse, because several disciplinary offences were heaped upon his shining head.

But it was an ensuing, albeit similar performance, which caught the public's eye, because on that occasion the Press found out.

The preliminaries were very similar to Max's unintentional train journey because he had been working another night shift, complete with clock, cushion and coffee, and at six o'clock had failed, yet again, to appear when it was time to book off duty.

Once again, the customary search was launched, and this time we included all the coaches at the railway station but without result. Every one of Max's known sleeping spaces was checked plus a few unknown ones, but he had vanished completely.

The panic and concern this time were at a level considerably lower than upon his railway trip, but there *was* concern and there *was* worry. This time he had vanished without a trace.

As worry increased, tension mounted and a larger search was authorized. The police dogs were called out, and radio-equipped vehicles brought in from other divisions. There was a total complement of about twenty men, so that a complete search of the town could be effected. It is fair to say that by 11.30 that morning everyone was worried, and even the stolid Polly was beginning to show some concern. He was now 5½ hours overdue. Her concern, however, arose because today was his day off, and he had arranged for her to knock him up at ten o'clock, after only some three hours sleep, so he could go fishing on the River Swale. That, she said, would have made him come off duty on time, and for that reason she was worried. She showed her anxiety by coming into town to join the search.

The sudden influx of police officers, vehicles and dogs, and their urgent enquiries around the town, soon came to the notice of the local reporter, who flashed the news to his friends on the national papers. The rapid arrival of several reporters from the nationals with their photographers, happened to coincide with Polly's decision to join the search. She was pictured with a worried frown as she made a token inspection of a boilerhouse – a lovely human-interest photograph.

By noon, the regional and national programmes were pumping out the story of Strensford's missing constable, and there is little doubt that the whole town, resident and visitor alike, knew of our very genuine concern. This time we were very worried, and the public joined the hunt. The locals knew where to look for Max, but failed to find him, while the visitors searched the most unlikely places, such as caves on the beach and deserted wood-land glades.

Eventually the time had arrived for the harbour to be dragged. There had a grown a nagging fear that the large constable, weighted down by his heavy uniform, might have slipped into the tidal waters and been drowned as the powerful undercurrents dragged him below. A few tentative searches of the waterline had been made, but there was nothing that resembled the soggy mess of a waterlogged Max.

To the delight of the newsmen, the Superintendent made the decision to drag the harbour. This would provide a marvellous seaside angle to the hunt and would produce some suitably dramatic pictures. As we had no marine section of the Force, he sought the help of the local fishermen. But they were not available either, because they were out of the harbour, fishing steadfastly somewhere on the grey North Sea. This meant we had to seek the assistance of some men who manned the pleasure boats. These were small cobles with a motor engine; they could carry a dozen folks out to sea, around the buoy and back again for a few shillings each.

Several of them offered to cruise up and down the harbour dragging the fearsome-looking grappling irons; we kept those at the station for such occasions. And so the search gathered momentum. As it did, so our concern, both official and private, steadily increased.

By two, I was due to book off duty, but every one of us volunteered to remain at work until Max was found, however long it took. By chance, I was parading an area at the top of Captain's Pass where the hotels had underground cellars. I had to check every one of them, and as I made my methodic searches I was worrying about Max's awful fate. I could see the harbour, and the little boats dragging their grappling irons. This made me think of the fishermen . . . suppose they netted his corpse or found him floating out to sea . . . The fishing boats, British and foreign, had gone out of the harbour this morning at high tide, some time before 5.30 a.m.

And those boats had very comfortable cabins . . . and those cabins were open at night . . .

As my mind followed those thoughts, I guessed where Max could be. It was the only answer. I walked along the clifftop to the coin-operated telescope which stands for the use of visitors but, before using it, looked out to sea with my naked eyes. I had no idea how far those boats travelled before dropping their nets, but if they were within sight of the shore, they could be seen with the telescope. Together, they would look like an armada or a small floating town, but I couldn't see them with my unaided vision.

As I was about to press a 3d bit into the telescope's coin box, I noticed Sergeant White walking briskly up Captain's Pass. He had not seen me, so I put my fingers to my mouth and produced a piercing whistle which he heard. I beckoned for him to join me.

'Now, young Rhea, what's up?' he asked when he joined me, slightly breathless after his steep climb up the cliff-face steps.

I explained my theory, and he smiled with quick understanding.

'The daft bugger!' he said, smiling at the thought. 'You'll be right, lad. He'll have gone below deck for a kip; he'll be somewhere near Dogger Bank now . . .'

'I wondered if we could check with this telescope?' I said. 'I was about to look when I saw you.'

'Go on, then."

I pressed my 3d bit into the slot, put my eye to the eyepiece and waited for the internal shield to move aside.

When the view cleared and I began my 3d worth of sight-seeing, I could make out a clutch of fishing vessels some distance off shore. I had no idea how far out to sea they were, but the quality of this telescope was insufficient to identify anything clearly. I could not even decide whether the boats in view were those from Strensford or the visiting foreign fleet.

'Hang on,' said Chalky White when I told him. 'I'll go across to the Imperial and ring the coastguard.'

I continued to watch until my money expired, and when I removed my eye from the telescope, I was surprised to find that a party of people had assembled around me.

'Is he out there?' someone asked, coming forward with his money. 'On those boats?'

'We're just checking,' I said. 'But feel free,' and I indicated the vacant telescope. Now we had a new tourist attraction in town – spot the constable. I stood aside as a longer queue formed; based on the theory that British can't resist queuing, everyone wanted to see what I'd been looking at. Such is human curiosity.

From regular visits to the Coastguard Station, I knew that the coastguards in their look-out high on the cliff at the opposite side of the harbour had a remarkably powerful set of binoculars; they were supported by a strong pillar and were more like a powerful telescope. Sergeant White would be asking the duty coastguard to examine those ships or even to make contact with them, to see if Max was on board.

It took a few minutes, by which time a growing crowd had gathered around my telescope as word passed among them. I wondered what they all expected to see, but when they saw Sergeant White returning with a smile, they all looked at him with expectancy.

'He's there,' he said, with a mixture of anger and relief. 'The silly . . . er . . .' He hesitated as he realized the crowd was hanging onto every word. 'Er . . . the silly fellow's there. He's on a Polish ship, the *Piaski*, and they've got him working. They don't like policemen in Poland, you see, and thought he was a spy. And they make stowaways work! So he's swilling the decks . . .' and he burst out laughing. 'They have refused to come all this way back with him. The coastguard's been in touch. So he'll have to stay there until the fleet comes home. The Poles knew nothing of the search of course. Serve him right . . . Well, folks,' he addressed the crowd. 'There he is, see if you can find him. It makes good viewing.'

And we left the growing crowd as we went into the Imperial Hotel to use their phone to ring the police station.

Mrs Cooper was very philosophical. 'Mebbe that'll put him off fishing,' was her only comment, as she awaited the headlines in tomorrow's papers.

Max was fined seven day's pay for that escapade, but he also became something of a folk hero. The town still talks about the night sleepy Max Cooper dreamt he was fishing – and woke up on the North Sea to find that he was.

10

And young and old come forth to play
On a sunshine holiday

John Milton, 1608–74

Because our brief spell of duty at Strensford was specifically to cope with the seasonal influx of holiday-makers, it was probable that we saw more of those than we did of the local people. There was very little time to form personal relationships or to know the residents.

This might have given a false image of the town and its population, but we did find that the visitors, whether they were there only for the day or for longer periods, were a friendly bunch of folks. The only regular trouble came from youths who grew rather boisterous after drinking too much, and from a few confidence tricksters who left their hotels and boarding houses without paying. And thoughtless motorists were a constant irritation.

Generally, those who took the trouble to journey to this corner of north-east England were a colourful, happy and fun-loving people, and as I walked that summer beat among them, I did experience several twinges of regret. That regret was my own wife and four tiny children could not be here too, that they could not enjoy the sands, the sea and the sunshine. I'd bring them later, I promised myself; it was such a charming place. Olde-worlde in many aspects, it had a powerful character of its very own, a character moulded by generations who had earned a tough living from the sea. That Strensford is picturesquely situated is never in doubt, for it is supported by some of England's finest and most dramatic countryside.

But if circumstances forced me to concentrate upon the visitors, they did not prevent me from noticing Edwin Dowson, a local man. Edwin was a man of routine, a life-long Strensford resident who was now well into his seventies, a gnomelike figure with a mop of iron-grey hair over his sharp little face.

Edwin's daily routine comprised a walk into the town centre and a visit to the Lobster Inn. He'd been a groomsman in his younger days and had worked for one of the Strensford major shipping families. Now that he was retired, Edwin followed his routine every weekday, beginning at 10.30 a.m. He concluded his first session at 2.30 p.m. This allowed him time to get his breakfast, tidy his cottage and walk into town. In town, he went to the bar of the Lobster and sat on his own chair in his own corner where he remained until closing time. He drank very little but he did enjoy the companionship of locals and visitors alike who drank in the same bar. Every weekday Edwin lunched at that pub. And then at night he performed a similar exercise. He left home at 7 p.m., walked down to the Lobster and left at 10.30 p.m., when it was closing-time. On the way home, he bought fish and chips.

He did his own shopping during the afternoons when the pub was shut, and on Sunday his routine varied slightly to accommodate the change in the licensing hours. But he never missed a day at the Lobster, and his routine never altered, day in, day out, year in, year out.

That is, until one day that summer.

It was a Saturday morning, and I was making my point at a telephone kiosk on the New Quay, just around the corner from the Lobster Inn. I knew that Edwin would be walking past at that time, for he left home prompt at 10.30 a.m. and arrived at the pub at 10.40 a.m. That was his weekday routine and it never varied.

When he failed to walk past, I grew a little worried. After all, he was well into his seventies and he did live alone, and so I wondered if he might have suffered some illness during the night. I walked to the door of the bar, which always stood open during the summer months, and peeped in. Edwin was not in his usual corner, and so I decided I should visit his little cottage, just to check on his welfare.

I climbed through the town via the steep steps which riddled the knots of red-roofed cottages as they clung so precariously to the cliffs which overlooked the harbour. High among the cluster of houses, I found his pretty little home. It was a one-up and one-down cottage and it was sandwiched between others of similar style. I knocked, but there was no reply and so I peered inside. It's very neat and tidy appearance suggested it was unoccupied. I hammered again, in case he was in bed, and then a door opened at the adjoining house.

'Yes?' said a lady in a flowered apron. 'Is it him you're after?'

'Yes. I'm just checking. I haven't seen Edwin this morning,' I explained. 'I wondered if he was all right.'

'Aye, he's fine,' she said, wiping her hands on the apron. 'He's gone on his holidays. Took a taxi at half eight this morning, loaded down with two suitcases, he was. He's gone for a fortnight.'

'Well, that's a relief. Where's he gone?'

'Dunno,' she said. 'He just went off with all his stuff.'

I thanked her for her help and returned to my beat. I must admit I was very relieved, and I thought no more about Edwin for some five or six days.

It was a hot Friday night, the town was very busy, and I was performing a half-night shift, that is from 5 p.m. until 1 a.m. I was working a harbourside beat, and the place was thronged with people enjoying the balmy air. Some time after nine o'clock, a group of youngsters in one of the pubs started a fight in which several glasses were broken, and I managed to quell that; then two other fights started at another pub, and it was evident it was going to be one of those nights. It threatened to be a duty interspersed with many minor scuffles. This sort of thing wasn't regarded as serious trouble, it was just a nuisance, and I coped. A lot of credit must go to the good humour of all concerned, including the local people. We, and the landlords, knew that the heavy hand of the law, or swift, hard retaliation from the locals, could stir up real bother. We humoured our visitors, we jollied them along, and nothing serious broke out.

Then Sergeant Blaketon met me at half-past ten. I was patrolling the quayside when I noticed his impressive figure in the light of a street lamp.

'Now, Rhea, anything doing?' he asked.

I told him about the scuffles in the various pubs and said that things were now under control.

'Right,' he said. 'Then we'll do a few pub visits.' He checked his watch. 'It's closing time now, so we'll clear them quickly and show our uniforms at the same time, just to prevent any bother later on.'

Together we patrolled all the quayside inns, checked a few youngsters' ages and cleared the bars of late drinkers. In most cases the landlords were pleased to see us, and we did get all the drinkers out. One or two continued to sing in the streets, and most of them wended their way home in an alcoholic haze. For them, life was wonderful – until morning!

The last inn on our tour was the Lobster. By that time it was almost eleven o'clock, and obviously word of our presence had got around because, when we entered, the bar was empty – except for one man. He was sitting there with a large pint in his fist.

I looked, and looked again. It was Edwin.

But Sergeant Blaketon spoke first.

'You!' he almost shouted at the little fellow. 'It's closing time, and you are drinking after hours! Give me that drink. Landlord!'

The surprised landlord emerged from the back of the bar, wiping a glass as he came towards us.

'Landlord, it is half-an-hour past closing time, and this man is still drinking. That is an offence,' Sergeant Blaketon began to lay down the law. 'It is an offence to serve after time, an offence to drink after time, and an offence . . .'

'No, it isn't, sergeant.' The landlord spoke softly, not flinching an inch before the might of Oscar Blaketon. 'Not in this case. Edwin is a resident. The licensing hours do not apply to residents.'

'What's your name?' barked Sergeant Blaketon to Edwin.

Edwin told him.

'Address?'

And Edwin gave his address, a matter of ten minutes from the pub.

'No, he's not, landlord,' said Blaketon in triumph upon learning Edwin's home address. 'That is the oldest trick in the world – you can't trick old stagers like me, you know. Oh no! Getting late drinkers to sign in as residents and get their names in the register. You ought to know better.'

'I am staying here,' piped up Edwin. 'I've booked in for two weeks.'

And he had. Blaketon insisted on seeing his room, but Edwin was right. This was his holiday. Because all his friends were here and because he liked the food, Edwin had simply come down to his favourite inn for two weeks holiday, when his food and bed would be provided, his washing-up and cleaning done for him, and his bed made every day. For Edwin, this was bliss.

'There's no point in going somewhere that's strange, is there, constable?' he looked up at me. 'I mean, what's the good of going on holiday where you don't know anybody? Besides,' he added, with a twinkle in his eye. 'I can drink late, can't I?'

It would be only two weeks later when a party from a Working Men's Club at Sunderland descended on the town. They came in two coach-loads, which meant there was around eighty of them, and they had consumed several crates of beer on the way to Strensford. Their mission in Strensford that Saturday evening appeared to be to consume as much local ale as they could, and this was to be achieved by visiting as many pubs as possible. Afterwards, they would catch their buses home. Those who could not walk to the buses would be carried by their pals. They would not see much of Strensford's quaint beauty and historic features, but that did not appear to bother them. They poured out of their buses at seven o'clock and marched purposefully towards the nearest pub. And so their mammoth binge began.

We were alerted and all the duty constables kept a discreet eye on their activities, knowing that after closing time we would have to act rather like sheepdogs as we shepherded them all safely to their waiting coaches.

And so we did. By the end of their marathon boozing session, they had split into little groups, and so by closing time all the pubs were evicting specimens of the working men of Sunderland. They were in various stages of intoxication, ranging from the merry to the legless, but they were no trouble. They were a happy, cheerful lot who couldn't remember where their buses had been parked, and so we, as expected, guided them to the coach-park.

I was one of the constables who had been allocated this task, and it was a laugh a minute getting them all into their seats.

When almost all were on board, I saw two men, both exceedingly merry, wending their way towards us.

'Howway, Jack, Eddie, man. We're waiting – get a move on!' called someone from one of the buses.

The one called Eddie was legless, speechless and clueless and was being stoutly supported by his pal.

'Eddie was on the other bus!' said his pal Jack with difficulty as he approached the open door.

'Never mind which bus he came on, man, get him on this yan, and you. It's time we were moving – an' we've ten crates of ale to finish afore we get yam.'

I stepped forward to help the near-unconscious Eddie on board. He was a huge man with a loud-checked jacket which was obviously new. We had difficulty getting him up the stairs and along the narrow aisle, but we succeeded, and he flopped onto a seat, where he promptly fell asleep.

It was with considerable relief that we watched those coaches depart from our area.

When I went into the police station to book off duty at a few minutes before one o'clock, Sergeant Blaketon was at the counter dealing with a distraught woman. I did not hear what she was saying, but as I walked in, he hailed me.

'Ah, PC Rhea,' he addressed me by my rank in the presence of a member of the public. 'You've been on the quayside and thereabouts all evening, haven't you?'

'Yes, sergeant,' I said.

'Well, this is Mrs Turnbull, and her husband has gone missing. She tells me they arrived at Strensford only this afternoon for a week's holiday, and this evening her husband went out for a drink. She didn't go with him because she was tired, and so she stayed behind at her lodgings . . .'

'He likes his drink, ye see, officer, but he canna swim a stroke,' she said in her strong Geordie accent. 'Man, he's so daft, ye knaw. Ah've never got him away on holiday before. Not the once. Ah had neea end of bother getting him doon here, he disna like leaving his mates, you knaw. And I bought him a lovely new jacket for the trip . . .'

'Where are you from, Mrs Turnbull?' I asked.

'Whey, Sunderland, man.'

'And your husband's name and description?'

'It's Eddie, and he's a big man, bigger than any of youse polis.'

'Is he a member of the Working Men's Club in Sunderland?' I asked.

'Whey, aye, man. They're all his pals. How is it you knaw all this then?'

'He's gone back to Sunderland,' I said. I tried to explain that the men wouldn't realize Eddie was here with his wife; when they encountered him in one of the pubs, they'd naturally think he was on their outing and, being mates, they'd made sure he got home safely.

'Ah canna win wi' that feller, can Ah?' she was in tears. 'When Ah think of all the bother Ah had to get him here, and now he's forgotten he was here with me! By, lad, Ah'll knock the living daylights out of him when Ah get back . . .'

'He is safe,' I said gingerly. 'At least he's not come to any harm.'

'Not for this week!' she growled as she stalked out of the station. 'He can stew at home. I'll stay here and enjoy myself without that silly bugger. Ah'll deal with him when Ah get back!'

'You know, Rhea,' said Sergeant Blaketon when she'd gone, 'Maybe that Eddie wasn't so drunk after all.'

Thinking about it later, I tended to agree. He would probably have a very happy holiday in Sunderland.

My most enduring memory of those weeks involved the most traditional of seaside sights – a small child playing with a bucket and spade on the sands.

It began when I was working a 9 a.m. to 5 p.m. shift in the town centre, a rare treat for any policeman because it meant he did not have to rise at the crack of dawn, neither did he have to work until late at night. It was a pleasure to be on duty. I walked slowly from the police station, savouring the warmth of the sunny day and the pleasing sight of casually dressed holiday-makers, especially the lovely girls.

As I passed the railway station, I noticed that one of the seaside-special trains had just pulled in. It was disgorging its complement of passengers into the town, and they were spilling out across the roads and pavements. I stood and watched, not for any particular reason, although it was nice to see their happy faces and relaxed behaviour. I was not studying the crowd, nor indeed observing them in the police sense, but I did notice a tiny girl with her blonde hair neatly plaited in two long tails. At the time, I did not know why she caught my attention, but she did. Maybe it was her demeanour or her long plaits? There was no reason to observe her. Nonetheless, I watched her walking beside several other people, and she was clutching a red bucket and a tiny spade with a blue blade. Together with the others, she crossed the road outside the railway station and followed the crowd towards the beach, a good ten minutes walk away.

Having seen the dispersal of that train-load, I went about my daily task of keeping traffic on the move, acting as unofficial guide and instant information service and generally attending to the multiplicity of minor tasks that came my way. My beat took me down to the harbourside, where I enjoyed the sunshine, the scent of the sea air and the eternal cry of wheeling gulls. If all police duty was like this, I could be very content.

Then a pretty, tanned woman in a suntop and shorts hailed me.

'Oh, thank goodness I've found you,' she said. 'I've found a little girl. I think she's lost.'

'Where is she?' I asked, for the woman was alone.

'I left her in the souvenir shop just around the corner.'

'I'll see to her,' I promised and hurried along to the shop in question.

We operated a well-oiled routine for dealing with lost children – dozens became separated from their parents during the season, and we never failed to re-unite any of them. More often than not, the child would be placed in the beach superintendent's hut, and in time an anxious parent would arrive to claim him or her. Those found wandering nearer the town centre were usually taken to the police station, where we kept a store of toys and games to amuse them until the worried parents turned up. So a lost child was not a real problem; some were a positive delight.

With the tanned woman at my side, I went into the shop and found the child seated on a high stool. She was sucking an iced lolly and I recognized her as the little girl I'd noticed leaving the railway station.

'Hello,' I said. 'And who are you?'

'Janice,' she said, sucking the lolly without any show of concern.

'And where do you live?'

'Number 42 Tayforth Street.'

'Which town is that?' I continued.

'Don't know,' she told me disarmingly.

'And where did you lose your mummy and daddy?' I said.

'I didn't lose them,' she sucked happily. 'I didn't have them.'

'You didn't have them?' I puzzled. 'What do you mean, Janice?'

'They never came. I came by myself.'

I halted in my questioning and now realized why she had been so prominent during my initial sighting of her. She had been walking alone; she had not been with anyone, not holding hands or being bustled along by anxious parents. She'd simply attached herself to some adults and children and had followed them . . . I could see it all now. It had meant nothing to me at that first sighting; now it meant everything.

'Janice, where do your mummy and daddy live?'

155

'With me, at home,' she said.

'No, I mean which town. You must know which town you live in.'

She merely shrugged her shoulders. At this the woman at my side attempted to gain this information.

'Janice, how old are you?'

'6¾,' she said.

'And which school do you go to?'

'Roseberry Road Infants,' she said without hesitation.

'That's in Middlesbrough,' the woman told me. 'I'm from Middlesbrough, but I've never heard of Tayforth Street. I wonder if it's on that new council estate?'

'What's your other name, Janice?' I asked.

'Massey,' she said. 'Janice Massey.'

'And you came to Strensford all by yourself?'

'Yes,' she said. 'I want to see the sands and the sea and dig sand castles.'

'Do your mummy and daddy know you've come?'

She shook her head. 'They couldn't bring me, so I came by myself. I'm all right.'

My heart sank.

'What about your money?' I put to her. 'How did you pay the man for coming on the train?'

'No, he never asked. I walked near other children.'

'And you walked near other children when you got here?' I asked.

She nodded. 'Then I got lost. I'm looking for the sands, so I can dig my castles.'

'You nearly got there,' I smiled. 'But look, I'll have to take you to the police station, and we'll have to tell your mummy and daddy where you are. They'll be very worried. Then I'm sure they will come and take you to see the sea and to dig castles on the sands.'

'All right,' and I helped her off the high stool. She was so light and fragile; she looked almost undernourished, but she was a pretty child with blue eyes and that long blonde hair. But at close quarters she needed a good bath; her hair was full of dirt and needed a thorough washing. Her pale skin was grimy too.

Her cheap, thin little dress was crumpled and poor, and on her feet were a pair of sandals which were almost worn out. I began to wonder about her background.

I thanked the shopkeeper for taking care of her and also the woman who'd found her, and told them both that I'd take her to the police station. There she would be fed, and there were those games we kept for such occasions, and while she was there, we would ask Middlesbrough Police to locate the parents and ensure they collected her.

Janice held my hand tightly as we walked through the town, and she kept asking me where the sea was and which way she would have to go to find it. I told her but said that first we had to tell her parents. As a small consolation, I took her along the harbourside and showed her the fishing boats and pleasure cruisers, and she loved the gulls which settled on the pavements and roads, seeking titbits from visitors.

She would not say a lot about herself, except that she had no brothers or sisters, and dad and mum were out all day. She did not know what her dad did for a living, or whether her mum earned any money, but it seemed they were both out of the house when she left home at morning. But Middlesbrough Police would find them – the neighbours would know their whereabouts. I felt very confident about that.

I took her into the dark depths of Strensford police station where Sergeant Blaketon was the duty sergeant.

'Hello, what's this, Rhea? A new girl-friend?'

'Yes, sergeant,' I smiled, still holding Janice's hand. 'This is Janice. She's come all the way from Middlesbrough without her mummy and daddy.'

'Has she, by jove? And why has she done that?'

'I want to see the sea,' piped Janice. 'And dig sand castles.'

'Hmm, well, what about your mummy and daddy then?'

I explained the circumstances and he rubbed his chin.

'All right, well, Rhea, you've done your bit. Now it's down to us. You go back to your beat and we'll find something for Janice to do while we find her mum and dad.'

I bade farewell to the child, and she smiled at me as Sergeant Blaketon took her into the office. There he would leave her in the capable charge of the office constable who would ring Middlesbrough Police to set in motion the search for her parents and her eventual collection.

If they'd arrived home and found her missing, they'd be frantic with worry, but from what she'd told me, they would have no idea she'd undertaken this journey.

I returned to my beat and patrolled the town until it was lunch-time.

I booked off at one o'clock and saw that Janice was having a meal supplied by a nearby café; she was on a tall stool in the main office with her plate on the counter, and she seemed quite content. At least there were no tears, and she seemed to be enjoying the food.

Three-quarters of an hour later, I returned to report that I was resuming my patrol – our lunch breaks were of forty-five minutes duration precisely. But Sergeant Blaketon called me to one side for a chat before I left for the town.

'Nicholas,' he said, and his use of my Christian name made me wonder what was coming next. 'That little girl, Janice. We've traced her parents – as we thought, they had no idea she'd come on that train. Now, her dad is at work until six tonight and he hasn't got a car. He's a warehouseman in Middlesbrough. Mum's a part-time voluntary worker in an old folks' home – she gets nothing for it, and it seems the family is not well off. Anyway, they'd arranged for young Janice to go to her granny's today – but she hadn't. Granny wasn't unduly worried when she didn't turn up because Mrs Massey sometimes changes her mind about going to the old folks' place, and the parents thought the child was at granny's.'

I listened to his long story, and wondered what he was coming to.

'Well,' he said. 'The outcome of all this is that her father will have to borrow a friend's car tonight, after work, to come here for her. There are no trains or buses into Strensford from Middlesbrough after six.'

'I'm pleased we've found them, anyway. So she'll have to hang about here until, well, nearly eight o'clock tonight?' I said. 'That's a hell of a long time for the child.'

'Exactly,' he confirmed. 'Which is the point of this conversation. Now, she likes you, so she tells me, she thinks you are kind. And young Rhea, you are a family man.'

I waited for his next suggestion.

'That little bairn has come all this way all by herself just to see the sea and build sand castles; she's even got her bucket and spade ready, but she's been sat in our office for hours already, waiting. Just waiting as good as gold. And with never a sniff of the sea or a sight of the beach.'

And I do believe I caught a tremor of emotion in his voice, and just a hint of moisture in his dark eyes. I had never seen him like this before.

'Yes, sergeant,' I agreed with him, for I did feel sorry for the little girl.

'So, go back to your digs, get changed into something light, the sort of stuff you'd wear on the beach if you took your own kids, and then come back here and take young Janice for a holiday on the sands,' the words tumbled from him; it was almost as if he didn't believe he was uttering them.

'As part of my duty, you mean?' I was amazed that he, of all the supervisory officers would take me away from uniform duties for a joyful task of this kind.

'Of course, Rhea. But be back no later than eight tonight – that's when her parents are due, and it'll be too late for them to take her onto the sands. We can't let her go home without making a sand castle, can we?'

I had some holiday clothes with me, and I did as he suggested. With little Janice carrying her precious bucket and spade and clutching my hand, I took her down to the seaside.

As I would have done with my own children, I helped her build castles, dams and holes in the smooth, warm sand; I gave her rides on the donkeys and we hunted for jellyfish, starfish and crabs in the rockpools. We found seaweed, shells and rounded stones which she loved, and there was a Punch and Judy show which she thoroughly enjoyed. I took her into an ice-cream parlour for a treat and showed her the lighthouse, the lifeboat and even the machines in the amusement arcades. But the sea and the sands were her great love – we went back and she paddled at the water's edge and allowed me to dry her feet on a towel I'd brought. Not once did she complain or misbehave. She was a lovely child, and by six o'clock both she and I were shattered.

We sat and let the hot sand run through our toes, and then she filled her little bucket with her collection of shells and rounded stones.

Shortly afterwards, from a kiosk close to the beach, I telephoned my landlady to ask if I could bring a lady-friend in for high tea and she agreed. When she met Janice and heard the story, she treated the little girl just like an important guest.

By eight the child was almost asleep on her feet. I gave her a piggy-back to the police station, and when we arrived, her parents were already there. Sergeant Blaketon was there too, having returned to make sure they did come for their child. I was more than delighted that they welcomed her with kisses and open arms, rather than subject her to an angry telling-off. I suspect Sergeant Blaketon had something to do with that, and she went happily to her parents. It was clear that they loved her, and that she loved them.

From her father's arms, she flung her thin hands around Sergeant Blaketon's neck and kissed him, and then she did the same to me.

'Thank you for taking me to the sands,' she said. 'I love you.'

And then she was gone.

She must be getting on for thirty now. She is very probably a very beautiful woman. I often wonder if she remembers that day with a constable by the sea.